Moses Dickson

Ritual of Taborian Knighthood

Moses Dickson

Ritual of Taborian Knighthood

ISBN/EAN: 9783337286729

Printed in Europe, USA, Canada, Australia, Japan

Cover: Foto ©Andreas Hilbeck / pixelio.de

More available books at **www.hansebooks.com**

RITUAL

—: OF :—

Taborian Knighthood,

——: INCLUDING :——

THE UNIFORM RANK.

———◆

ST. LOUIS, MO.:
A. R. FLEMING & CO., PRINTERS.
1889.

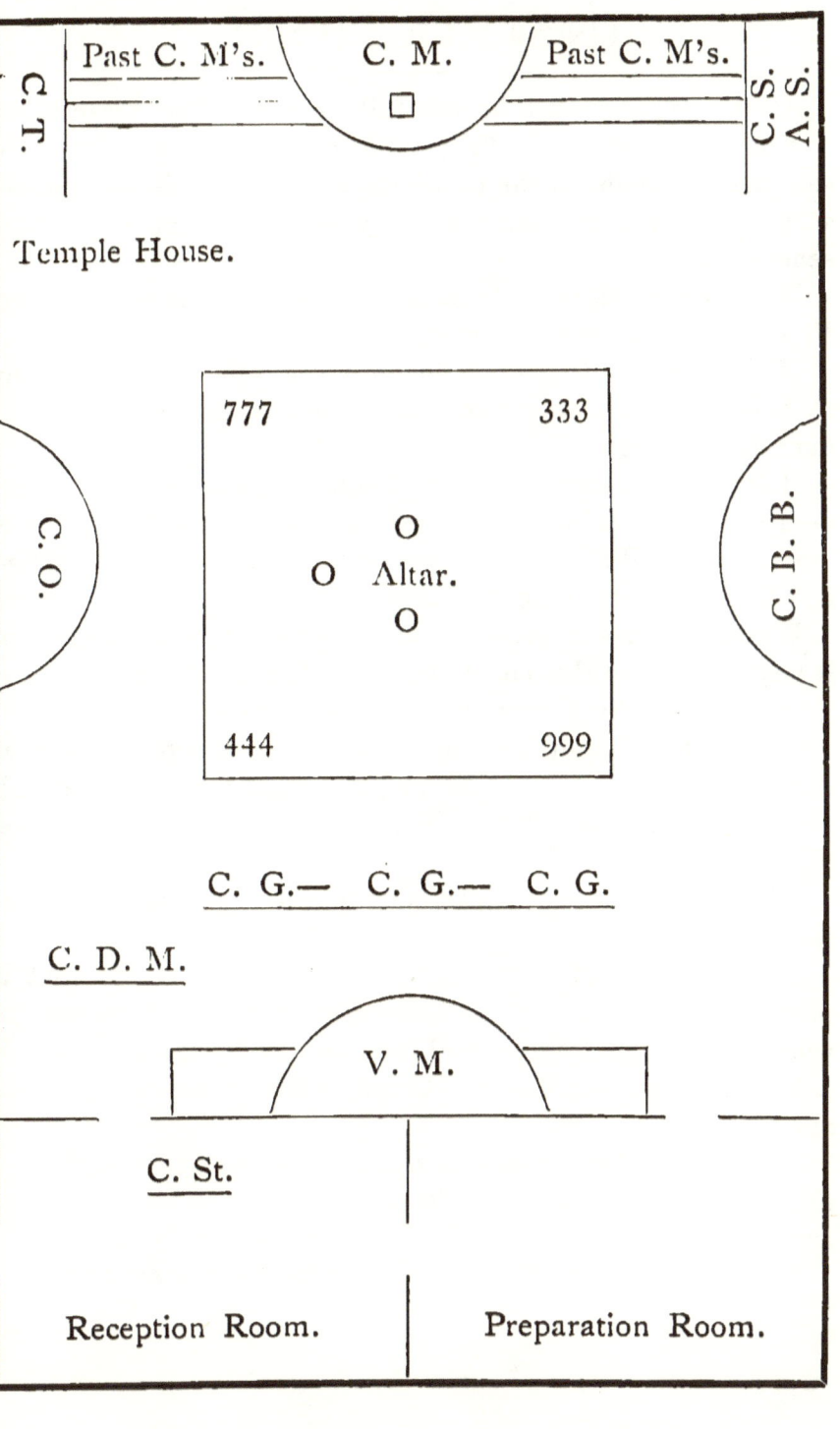

INSTRUCTIONS.

All the degrees must be carefully given. The ceremonies and degrees ought to be fully followed so that a good impression may be made on the candidate's mind. It is not necessary to use the candidate roughly—this will not impress a sensible man.

If the First Degree is to be given, open the Temple in the First Degree in regular form.

If the Second Degree is to be given, open the Temple in that degree. A candidate will be better instructed by not hurrying through.

If the Third Degree is to be given, open the Temple in that degree. The candidate in the preparation room will note these movements. While he may not understand them, he is satisfied that it is something for his benefit.

When the three degrees are to be given at one meeting, it is best to open in the Third Degree. The C. M. can call the Temple to rest by giving three raps—all stand.

C. M.—Sir Knights, by the authority in me vested, I now declare. . . . . .Temple, No. . . . . ., from work to rest until further notice. Sir D. M., please give this notice to the C. St.

C. M. gives one rap, which calls to order, and the officers to their stations.

C. M.—Sir D. M., please give notice to the C. St. that I propose to call. . . . . .Temple, No. . . . . ., from rest to work in the First Degree, and instruct him to do his duty.

C. D. M. to C. M.—Sir Chief, your orders have been obeyed.

C. M. gives three raps—all stand. I now declare and proclaim. . . . . .Temple, No. . . . . ., opened in the First Degree for work—one rap. Sir D. M., please notify the C. St.

C. D. M.—Sir Chief, your orders have been obeyed.

4

In the same manner each House is called from work to rest, and from rest to work, until the finish. The only business done in the first three Houses is the giving of the degrees. For regular or call business the Fourth House must be opened. No degrees are to be given at a regular monthly meeting, except in an absolute emergency.

The Regalia for the First Degree is a scarlet collar, cap lettered K. T., and a javelin and brown gloves. The C. M. and Past C. M's, pea green collar.

The Regalia for the Second Degree is a scarlet collar and apron, cap lettered T. D., brown gloves and javelin. C. M. and Past C. M's, pea green collar and apron.

The Regalia for the Third Degree is a scarlet collar and apron, a cap lettered T. D. P., a sword and scarlet belt, brown gloves. The C. M. and Past C. M's, pea green collar and apron.

The Regalia for the Fourth Degree is fully explained in the Ritual of the Rank.

The four degrees cannot be given at one meeting and do justice to the candidate. The first three degrees can be given. The Fourth Degree must be given at a meeting set apart for it alone. The length of the degree requires time.

The authority to organize Temples and Tabernacles is vested in the Chief Grand Mentor—C. G. M.—and his deputies, as follows: District Grand Mentors—D. G. M.; Deputy Grand Organizers—D. G. O.; Special Grand Deputy-Daughters— S. G. D.

See further instructions on the Fourth Degree on the page just before the Fourth Degree Lecture.

Secret Orders are organized for the express benefit of their members in case of sickness, distress, death, and to care for the widows and orphans of deceased members. The larger and more wide-spread the Order is, the greater should be its benefits. Each Temple and Tabernacle ought to keep a full treasury.

KNIGHTS OF TABOR
—o r—
FIRST DEGREE.

FORM OF OPENING.

At the proper hour the C. M. takes his seat and gives one rap. This calls the Knights to order and the officers and members to their seats.

C. M.—Sir Knights, we are preparing to open............ Temple, No....., in the First Degree. If there are any persons present that are not members of the Order, I will thank them to retire.

C. M. gives one rap. The C. D. M. advances to the Chief. The Chief says: Sir D. M., you will please to attend and receive the word and report.

C. D. M. to C. M.—Sir Chief, I have visited all, and find each person in full uniform with our Order.

C. M.—It is well. Sir D. M., you will please to place the C. St. at his post and invest him, inform him that we are ready to open............Temple, No....., and order him to let none enter or pass out until further orders from the Chief.

The C. D. M. places the C. St. outside of the door with instructions, closes the door and gives two raps, this is answered by the C. St. by two raps. C. D. M. gives one and C. St. answers by one.

The C. D. M. returns to the C. M. and says: Sir Chief, the C. St. is at his post with full instructions.

C. M.—It is well. Let us prepare in the regular form. (The officers, members and visitors put on their regalia.) The C. M. gives two raps and officers stand.

C. M.—Sir C. D. M., your duty in and about the Temple?

6

C. D. M.—My duty is to take charge of the inner door, to see that none pass or repass without permission from the Chief.

C. M. to C. D. M.—The C. St.'s post and duty?

C. D. M.—His post is at the outer door, duty to keep off all who are not members, take charge of and prepare the rooms for meetings.

C. M. to Sir C. G.—Your duty?   (1st Guard answers.)

Our duties are to assist the C. M. in giving degrees and preserve decorum during the hours of business.

C. M.—Sir C. T., your duty?

C. T.—My duty is to receive all money and money orders, pay all orders properly drawn, and have my books and papers always ready for inspection.

C. M.—Sir C. S., your duty?

C. S.—My duty is to keep a record of the doings of the Temple, collect all dues and other money belonging to the Temple, pay the same to the C. T., report quarterly to the C. G. M. and annually to the Grand Session.

Sir V. M., your duty?

V. M.—My duty is to assist the C. M. in his presence, and in his absence perform all his duties.

C. M.—Sir V. M. the C. M.'s duty?

V. M.—His duty is to preside at all meetings of the Temple, call special meetings when business requires it, decide all questions of rules and regulations, see that the by-laws of his Temple and the edicts of the Grand Temple and laws are strictly enforced, and represent his Temple at the Annual Sessions.

C. M.—Sir C. O., your duty?   (Gives three raps, all stand.)

C. O.—My duty is to conduct the devotional exercises of the Temple, visit and give consolation to the sick, and attend to the funeral services of Sir Knights and Daughters.

C. M.—Sir Knights, assemble in form. (They assemble on the square, face in.)

C. M.—Sir Knights, to the right-about face (deposit javelins), doff caps, left-about face, to your devotions.

The C. O. conducts as follows:

GOD'S GOODNESS. C. M.

Come, let us join, our Lord to praise,
Whose mercy knows no end;
To Him our cheerful voices raise,
Our father and our friend.

In tender infancy His care
Preserved our lives from harm;
And now He keeps us from the snare
Of sin's deceitful charm.

PRAYER.

O, Almighty God, who has built Thy Temple upon the foundation of Thy Almighty Power and Word. The Messiah Himself being the chief head of the corner stone, the rock and keystone of our faith. Grant that we may be so joined together in the unity of spirit by Thy teachings that we may be made an Holy Temple acceptable unto Thee, our Lord and Savior. Amen! Amen!! Amen!!!

C. M.—Sir Knights, right-about face, recover javelins, cover heads, to the left-about face, march to seats and stand.

C. M.—Sir Knights, assist me in the signs. (In the First Degree, the signs of that degree only are given.)

C. M.—I now proclaim.................Temple, No....., opened in the First Degree, in Friendship, Love and Harmony.

Sir D. M., you will notify the C. St. that.............. Temple, No....., is now open; and if there are any members of the Order that wish to enter, admit them by the inner door and pass of this degree.

BUSINESS.

The C. M. says: Sir Knights, we have opened to give the First Degree to Mr........................... We will thank you to assist us. Attention! C. G., you will now prepare the candidate and introduce him. The three C. G's repair to the adjoining room where the candidate is in waiting, and blindfold him, and conduct him into and around the hall once, and halt him in front of the Temple House, where the C. O. is standing.

The C. M. claps his hands and all rise to their feet. The candidate standing in front of the C. O. during the reading.

The C. O. reads as follows:

My son, if thou wilt receive my words, and hide my commandments with thee;

So that thou incline thine ear unto wisdom, and apply thine heart to understanding;

Yes, if thou criest after knowledge, and liftest up thy voice for understanding;

If thou seekest her as silver, and searchest for her as for hid treasures;

Then shalt thou understand the fear of the Lord, and find the knowledge of God.

The candidate is conducted around the Temple three times, and halted at the first square. He is placed on the number 777.

The C. O. speaks slowly, as follows:

My son, forget not my law, but let thy heart keep my commandments;

For length of days, and long life, and peace shall they add to thee;

Let not mercy and truth forsake thee; bind them about thy neck; write them upon the tablet of thy heart;

So shalt thou find favor and good understanding in the sight of God and man.

The candidate is carried by the Guards to the next square, 333, and, he standing on it, the C. O. speaks:

As a bird that wandereth from her nest, so is a man that wandereth from his place;

Ointment and perfume rejoice the heart; so doth the sweetness of a man's friend by hearty counsel;

Thine own friend, and thy father's friend, forsake not; go

into thy brother's house in the day of calamity, for better is a neighbor that is near than a brother far off;

All this I have proved by wisdom. I said, I will be wise, but it is far from me;

That which is far off, and exceeding deep, who can find it out?

I applied mine heart to know, and to search, and to seek out wisdom, and the reason of things.

The candidate is carried to the third square, 999, and, he standing on it, the C. O. speaks:

Let not mercy and truth forsake thee; bind them about thy neck; write them upon the tablet of thy heart;

So shalt thou find favor and good understanding in the sight of God and man;

They are all plain to him that understandeth, and right to them that find knowledge;

Receive my instruction and not silver, and knowledge rather than choice gold;

For wisdom is better than rubies, and all the things that may be desired are not to be compared with it;

Wisdom dwells with prudence, and finds out knowledge of witty inventions.

The candidate is carried to the fourth square, 444, and, he standing on it, the C. O. speaks:

Wisdom gives length of days in her right hand, and in her left hand riches and honor;

Her ways are ways of pleasantness, and all her paths are peace;

She is a tree of life to them that lay hold upon her, and happy is every one that retaineth her;

The Lord by wisdom hath founded the earth; by understanding hath He established the heavens;

By His knowledge the depths are broken up, and the clouds drop down the dew;

If thou sayest, behold, we knew it not; doth not He that pondereth the heart consider it? and He that keepeth thy soul, doth not He know it? and shall not He render to every man according to his works?

My son, eat thou honey, because it is good, and the honeycomb, which is sweet to thy taste;

So shall the knowledge of wisdom be unto thy soul; when thou hast found it then there shall be a reward, and thy expectation shall not be cut off.

C. O. to candidate.—You have passed every square. Remember the instructions and keep the advice given, and you will prosper in all your undertakings, and be an honored Brother among us. Sir Guards, you will conduct the candidate to the Temple House, and place him in proper position to take the obligation. The candidate is conducted slowly around the hall while the following is read. The V. M. reads as follows:

1. How long shall earth's alluring toys,
   Detain our hearts and eyes,
   Regardless of immortal joys,
   And strangers to the skies?

2. These transient scenes will soon decay,
   They fade upon the sight;
   And quickly will their brightest day
   Be lost in endless night.

The candidate is placed in front of the Temple House, his right hand raised palm out, with the *three evils* and *four good* standing behind him. The members standing with their toes touching the sides of the square. The C. M. administers the following obligation. He says to the candidate: Please repeat after me—

OBLIGATION.

"I, B. D., in the fear of the Lord, and in His presence, do, with sincere truth, promise that I will keep the secrets of the Order of (12) Twelve and those of a Brother Friend and Daughter of the Tabernacle.

"Furthermore, I promise that I will come to the call of every sign of a Brother Knight.

"Furthermore, I promise that I will contribute of my means to assist a Brother Knight in distress; I will advise and give him aid.

"Furthermore, I promise to obey all laws, rules and regulations of the Order of Twelve, and will be regular in attending all meetings of the Order.

"I further promise and swear that I will obey the call of every sign of a worthy Daughter of the Tabernacle.

"I promise and swear that I will aid and help a worthy Daughter of the Tabernacle in her distress, with my money, by advice, and use all honorable means to give aid.

"I further promise that I will defend the good name of a worthy Brother Knight and a Daughter of the Tabernacle wherever assailed, in any place and at any time.

"To all of which I do most earnestly promise and affirm, binding myself under the penalty of having my body quartered and consumed by fire. So help me Lord, and keep me firm."

SHOCK.

C. M. says.—Let the candidate see light; stretch out your hands and assist me. One—two—three—LIGHT. The bandage drops. The members are all seated, except the GOOD and EVIL. The C. M. tells the candidate to look! The first he sees are the *great evils*, which are thus explained:

ENVY.—(Envy dressed in a green robe with a green false-face; he walks to the front of the candidate and speaks)—I represent Envy; I come to teach an important lesson. The Great Dispenser of Gifts to Mankind has given to man as it pleases Him, and if you do not improve the talent He has given, and others do better than you do, do not envy them, but try to do your part in the great world you live in. To envy another the possession of anything is an evidence of a small mind and mean disposition—Envy walks slowly away.

FALSEHOOD.—(Falsehood is dressed in a black robe streaked with red; black false-face dotted with red; he walks slowly to the front of the candidate.)—I represent Falsehood. It tells of deceit, dishonesty, deception, untruthful and treacherous lying to mislead. I admonish you never to be guilty of a falsehood; no, never—Falsehood walks slowly away.

COVETOUSNESS.—(Covetousness is dressed in a white robe spotted with black. False-face spotted. Walks to the front of the candidate.)—I represent Covetousness. It means desire. It teaches you that it is not honorable to covet that which is another's, but in life's pursuits you should acquire wisdom, virtue, honor and friends. Remember the *three evils*. May they never be found in you—Covetousness walks away.

THE FOUR GOOD LESSONS.

The *four good* walk to the front of the candidate together. The C. M. explains as follows: Look at these, my friend, and learn what they teach—

JUSTICE.—Justice, covered with the white robe, represents the true and just that are innocent of all wrong-doing, and recommend that you remember it.

LOVE.—Love, covered with the blue robe, teaches you to love the Brother Knights as thyself, and that Love is the base of our Order, upon which the superstructure of Knighthood is built.

TEMPERANCE.—Temperance, in robes of drab, teaches you that you should have an even temper, and govern the mind, body and appetite.

TRUTH.—Truth, dressed in robes of scarlet, tells us of that Divine Being who proved His true friendship for man on Calvary's hill. It tells us to be true to a Brother Knight.

May you remember these four good lessons, and may Justice, Love, Temperance and Truth be your companions through life—They walk away.

C. M. to C. G.—You may conduct our Brother to the C. O. for further instruction.

The C. G. conducts the candidate around the hall, while the members sing as follows:

God gives us friends, who seek our good,
 And strive to make us wise;
His bounteous hand provides our food,
 And all our wants supplies.

They halt at the Chief Orator's station.

C. G. to C. O.—Sir Chief sends this new Brother to you for instruction in the language of the Temple.

C. O. to C. G.—The Chief's orders shall be obeyed. (To candidate.) You are about to be invested with the language of the Order, so as to make yourself known as a Sir Knight in any land or country, which you must not forget. Be careful and attentive to the instruction, for by it you will be known and received as a Brother Friend.

Brother and Friend, we speak by signs. The signs in the Degree of Tabor are the test signs, and are given as follows:

THE TEST.—The first sign is given by closing the three last fingers of your right hand, letting your elbow rest on your hip, the index finger this is the sign of admission and tells that I have been admitted and made a Knight of Tabor—this is also the saluting sign to be given when the Temple is open in the First Degree.

SECOND SIGN.—The sign of silence is given by laying the open left hand on the mouth, fingers pointing to the nose, this is the answering sign to the test, and tells that I am a Knight of Tabor, it is also a warning sign to warn a Knight that he is doing or saying something that will injure him, and it admonishes him to look well to what he is doing or saying.

SIGN OF DISTRESS.—The sign of distress is given by raising the right hand above your head, the thumb and two fingers open, and the last two fingers closed. This sign is given when you need counsel, aid or advice.

THE TOKEN.—This sign is given by advancing toward each other under the test sign, and grasping the fore finger of each other, the other fingers closed, and the thumbs pressed close to the hands, side by side, pointing to the wrist. The first says, *Firm.* The second says, *Friendship.* The first answers, *I greet you, Brother Friend.*

THE MEMORIAL WORD.—The scenes that were enacted around and about Mount Tabor 1296 years before the birth of Christ, were mainly instrumental in founding the Taborian Knighthood. In this, the First Degree, the pass-word that we use is TABOR. This word will admit you into a Temple that opens in the First Degree. You give this word if you are present when the Temple is opening in the First Degree.

C. O. to C. G.—Sir Guards, please conduct this Brother Friend to the Chief Mentor; he will give further instruction.

The C. G. conducts the Brother Friend once around the Temple Hall and halts in front of the C. M.'s station, and calls his attention by one rap on the floor with the Guard's javelin.

Sir Chief, the C. O. sends this Brother to you with proper instruction.

C. M.—Look well and bear your part of the chain that has no end. May you prove true to the obligations you have taken, for when they are once taken they ought never to be broken. They bind you for life to the Order of Twelve. I take pleasure in presenting to you this collar. The Guards will place it properly upon you. The color is scarlet, an emblem of zeal, and typical of firm friendship. May you zealously guard the good name of the Order of Twelve. Be firm and unchangeable in your frienship for every member.

I present to you this javelin. It is an instrument of war, used by the ancient Knights as a weapon of attack and defense. In the hands of those old warriors it was a terrible weapon, especially in a charge of armored soldiers when meeting in a hand-to-hand fight. It is to remind you that you have to defend a Brother Friend when he is in danger.

C. M. gives three raps, all stand. I now announce that H. A. has been regularly inducted into the First Degree of Tabor. He is now a Brother Friend, with all the honors of firm friendship; he is one of us in the bonds that must not be broken. C. G., please seat our Brother Friend. One rap seats all.

Lecture of the First Degree, or some part of it, must be rehearsed before closing in this degree.

LECTURE, FIRST DEGREE.

Q. Have we ever met before?

A. We may have, as we have traveled considerably.

Q. In what places have you traveled?

A. I have traveled in the land of Judea, and other historical places.

Q. Did you visit any mountains in Judea?

A. Yes; I have visited mountains in Judea.

Q. Can you name it?

A. Perhaps I can, with your assistance.

Q. You begin.

A. If you will tell me the last grand scene that transpired upon the mountain, I will give you the name.

Q. It was the transfiguration of the Messiah.

A. The name of that mountain is Tabor.

Q. What road did you travel to arrive at its summit?

A. I encircled the mount three times and passed every square.

Q. What was said to you at the first square?

A. It was said: My son, forget not my laws.

Q. What was said to you at the second square?

A. Thine own friend and thy father's friend forsake not.

Q. What was said to you at the third square?

A. I was told to seek out wisdom and the reason of things.

Q. What was said to you at the fourth square?

A. Behold, I build an house to the name of the Lord, my God, to dedicate it to Him. For great is our God above all gods.

Q. What further was done with you?

A. I was placed in front of the Temple House, where I took a solemn obligation, which makes me a Brother Friend.

Q. After the obligation what was done with you?

A. I was caused to see light.

Q. What did you first see?

A. Good and Evil.

Q. Can you name them?

A. I can, with your assistance.

Q. Do you know anything about evil?

A. Falsehood comes next.

Q. I was taught not to covet.

A. But to give justice—love a Brother Friend—be temperate in all things and speak the truth at all times.

Q. Have you the test?

A. I have been adopted.

Q. I am silent. ☞

A. Give me your hand, Brother. They give the grip and word.

Q. I am glad to meet you.

CLOSING.

If there is no further business, the Temple closes as follows:

C. M.—Sir Drill Master, you will please inform the Chief

Sentinel that............Temple, No....., now open in the
First Degree is about to close, to stand so until...........

The C. D. M. goes to the door and gives three raps. The C.
St. answers by three raps and opens the door just wide enough
to hear. The C. D. M. delivers the C. M.'s orders and closes
the door and gives one rap, the C. St. answers by one rap,
the C. D. M. returns to his station and reports.

Sir Chief, the C. St. is at the post with full instructions.

C. M.—I thank you. Attention, Brother Friends. Three
raps are given, and all stand and uncover.

C. O. delivers the following (or some other suitable)

PRAYER.

Almighty God, the preserver of all who trust in Thee, we
bless Thy great name for the mercies bestowed upon us and
for the harmony vouchsafed to us in our enclosure during this
meeting, and as we are now about to disperse let Thy mercies
continue with us, and guide us through life and in Heaven
save us. Amen! Amen!! Amen!!!

The signs in the First Degree are given from last to first.

C. M.—I now declare................Temple, No.....,
closed until............in Love, Friendship, Peace and Harmony. One rap. Sir Drill Master, please inform the Chief
Sentinel that the Temple is closed, to stand so until........

THE SECOND DEGREE
—O R—
THE DALMON LOCK.

It is opened the same as the First Degree, except the signs and pass-word.

THE DEGREE.

C. M.—Sir Knights, we have assembled to confer the Dalmon Lock on our Brother Friend............ I will thank you for your assistance. Sir D. M., you will please inquire if the candidate is in the ante-room. The D. M. goes to the door and gives three raps. The C. St. answers by three raps and partly opens the door.

C. D. M.—(Whispering.)—Are there any candidates in waiting?

C. St.—(Whispering.)—There are......in the preparation room. The door is closed and the usual raps given.

C. D. M.—(From his station.)—Sir Chief, I have inquired if there are candidates in waiting. I report that......are in the preparation room.

C. M.—Thank you. Sir Guards, you will now attend to the preparation of the candidates, and conduct them to the entrance door. The C. G's retire to the preparation room and prepare the candidates by blindfolding, and conduct them to the door, and give three loud knocks. The C. D. M. goes to the door and answers by three raps, and partly opening the door, asks:

Who are you, and why are you at the entrance of Dalmon Lock?

C. G.—(For candidate.)—I am a Brother Friend who desires to be instructed in true Knighthood.

C. D. M.—By what means did you get this far on your journey?

C. G.—(For candidate.)—I rode well, I stood well, I squared well and passed the Temple of the Knights of Tabor.

C. D. M.—Do you bring no word of greeting to tell of the past? Can you give it to me?

They give the grip. Candidate (prompted) says: I passed the Temple of Firm Friendship.

C. D. M.—It is well. I will conduct you to the C. M. for further instruction.

The C. D. M. receives and conducts the candidate around the room three times.

The Vice-Mentor reads:

> Lord, Thou hast searched and seen me through;
> Thine eye commands, with piercing view,
> My rising and my resting hours,
> My heart and flesh, with all their powers.
>
> My thoughts before they are my own
> Are to my God distinctly known;
> He knows the words I mean to speak,
> Ere from my opening lips they break.
>
> Within Thy circling power I stand,
> On every side I find Thy hand;
> Awake, asleep, at home, abroad,
> I am surrounded still with God.

The reading is so timed that at the end of the last verse they arrive in front of the C. M. and halt.

Sir Chief reads: Then Solomon began to build the house of the Lord of Jerusalem in Mount Moriah, where the Lord appeared unto David, his father, in the place that David had prepared in the threshing floor of Ornan, the Jebusite.

And he began to build the temple in the second day of the month, in the fourth year of his reign.

Now these are the things wherein Solomon was instructed for the building of the house of God. The length of cubits after the first measure was three score cubits, and the breadth twenty cubits.

And the porch that was in front of the house, the length of it was according to the breadth of the house, twenty cubits, and the heighth was an hundred and twenty, and he overlaid it within with pure gold.

And the greater house he sealed with fir tree, which he overlaid with fine gold, and set thereon palm trees and chains.

And he garnished the house with precious stones for beauty, and the gold was gold of Parvain.

He overlaid also the house with beams, the posts and the walls thereof, and the doors thereof with gold, and 'graved cherubims on the walls.

This is a brief history of the great temple built by King Solomon. The instruction he received came from the Supreme Master Builder of the World. The Temple we are building is in honor of Solomon's instructor; the material we are putting in our Temple must believe in and honor the Lord God, who was transfigured on Mount Tabor.

C. D. M.—(For candidate.)—I both honor and believe in the Lord, the Savior of mankind.

C. M.—You have spoken well. Sir D. M., you will now conduct the candidate to the Chief Orator for further instruction. As they pass around the hall, the V. M. reads the following, slowly:

But will God indeed dwell upon the earth? Behold, the Heaven and Heaven of Heavens cannot contain Thee; how much less this house that I have builded.

Yet have Thou respect unto the prayer of Thy servant, and his supplication, O Lord, my God, to hearken unto the cry and to the prayer which Thy servant prayeth before Thee to-day.

That Thine eyes may be open toward this house night and day, even toward the place of which Thou hast said, My name shall be there, that Thou mayest hearken unto the prayer which Thy servant shall make toward this place.

And hearken Thou to the supplication of Thy servant, and of Thy people, Israel, when they shall pray toward this place, and hear Thou in Heaven, Thy dwelling place, and when Thou hearest, forgive.

If any man trespass against his neighbor, and an oath be laid upon him to cause him to swear, and the oath come before Thine altar in this house.

Then hear Thou in Heaven, and do, and judge Thy servants, condemning the wicked to bring his way upon his head, and justifying the righteous, to give him according to his righteousness.

The reading is so timed that at the third round it is ended, and the D. M. and the candidate halts at the C. O.'s station.

D. M. to C. O.—Sir Orator, we have traveled by order of the Chief Mentor to find thee. We are seeking for instruction.

C. O.—By what means did you get thus far on your journey?

Candidate.—I rode well, I stood well, I squared well, and passed the Temple of the Knights of Tabor.

C. O.—Do you bring no word of greeting to tell of the past ? Can you give it to me?

Candidate.—I will give you that and what I received when I passed the Temple of Firm Friendship. Gives the grip.

C. O.—Come in, thou blessed of the Lord, stranger nor foe art thou; we welcome thee with warm accord, our Friend and Brother now.

The hand of fellowship, the heart of love, we offer thee.

Come with us; we will do thee good, as God to us hath done; stand but to Him, whose faith the victory won.

Witness, ye men and angels, now before the Lord we speak, to Him we make our solemn vow, a vow we dare not break.

C. O.—Sir D. M., it is my will that the candidate be conducted to the Temple House and placed in proper form to take the obligation of a Knight of Dalmon. The candidate is marched slowly around the hall, while the following is read by the C. O., each member repeating after him:

> The perfect world, by Adam trod,
> Was the first temple built by God;
> His fiat laid the corner stone;
> He spake, and lo! the work was done.

He hung its starry roof on high,
The broad expanse of azure sky;
He spread its pavement, green and bright,
And curtained it with morning light.

The mountains in their places stood,
The sea, the sky, and all was good;
And when its first pure praises rang,
The morning stars together sang.

Lord, 'tis not ours to make the sea,
And earth, and sky, a house for Thee;
But in Thy sight and off'ring stands
An humble temple, built with hands.

The members form in procession behind the candidate as he moves around. At the last verse the D. M. places the candidate in front of the Temple House, the Knights form a square around the candidate and C. O., the D. M. standing behind them. The right hand of the candidate is placed on the Bible, the left hand on his breast.

The D. M. advances to the C. M.'s post and says: Sir Chief, the candidate is placed in proper position to receive your instruction, I am ready to conduct you to the Temple House. The D. M. conducts the Chief to the letter "O" opposite the candidate.

C. M. to candidate.—You have succeeded as a Brother Friend in coming to the centre of Dalmon Lock. You cannot go farther, unless you take a binding obligation. Please give your full name, and repeat after me:

OBLIGATION.

I, A. O., in the presence of the Lord of Lords and these Brother Friends, do solemnly promise and swear that I will keep and conceal the secrets of this degree and those of my Brother Friends.

I further promise that I will obey all signs and summons given to me by the hand of a Sir Knight or Daughter of the Tabernacle.

I further promise that I will aid and assist any poor, indigent

Sir Knight or Daughter, they making application to me, I knowing them to be worthy, and if my ability permits.

To all of which I promise, binding myself to keep and perform the same, under no less a penalty than to have my right arm cut off, should I willfully violate this, my solemn obligation. Amen! (The members all repeat, Amen.)

C. M. to D. M.—Sir Drill Master, give the obligated Knight of Dalmon light. (The hoodwink is removed.)

C. M.—Sir Knights, another has been added to our ranks. Let us show him how strong the Dalmon Lock can be made to protect a Knight of Dalmon. (The chain is formed by crossing the right arm over the left and clinching each other's hands, thus forming an endless chain, with the newly obligated Knight in the centre.) Look around this endless chain and this solid wall, and be assured that the Knights of Dalmon will, like a living wall, form for your protection when in danger. Sir V. M., I have finished. (The C. M. returns to his post.)

V. M.—Sir Knights, attention! Unlock, and to the right-about face! March to seats!

C. O. to D. M.—Please conduct the obligated Knight to the Chief Mentor. (The D. M. conducts the Knight to C. M.)

D. M.—Sir Chief, the C. O. has obeyed your orders, and this obligated Knight is returned to you for the full instruction.

C. M.—Thank you. I take pleasure in giving this Knight of Dalmon the means of making himself known as a member of Dalmon Lock. Your love for the Order of Twelve is evident, for you have shown it by the desire you have to learn more of its work. You now want to fix your mind in love for the Order, and be zealous in fulfilling every duty. Hear the lesson and heed its instruction.

The C. M. reads:

> Zeal is that pure and heavenly flame
> The fire of love supplies;
> While that which often bears the name
> Is self in a disguise.

True zeal is merciful and mild,
  Can pity and forbear;
The false is headstrong, fierce and wild,
  And breathes revenge and war.
Self may its poor reward obtain,
  And be applauded here;
But zeal, the best applause will gain.
  Oh Lord, the idol of self dethrone,
And from our hearts remove;
  And let no zeal by us be shown,
But that which springs from love.

THE SECRET LANGUAGE.

C. M.—If you will give me your attention I will impart to you the secret means of making yourself known as a Knight of Dalmon. The first sign is—

THE ONWARD HAIL.—This sign is given with the right hand closed, thumb extended and elbow resting on the hip; hand waving three times, distinctly, to and fro. When you desire to ask if there are any members of the Knighthood present, you give this sign. It can be given at any time and in any place.

THE ANSWERING HAIL.—The sign of recognition is given by placing your right hand on your breast, thumb pointing to the chin. This sign answers the onward hail, and proves that he who gives it is a member of the Knighthood.

CALLING SIGN.—This sign is given by holding up your right hand, palm out, top of the fingers even with the right shoulder. The first motion—Turn the hand half around. Second motion—Turn palm inward. Third motion—Throw the hand over the right shoulder. This sign is given when wishing to call a Knight, but you are admonished not to use it unless you need the Knight's presence on something important.

THE TOKEN.—The token is given in this way: Two fingers in the palm of the right hand, hands closed.

The word is STAND.

The answer is TRUE.

SALUTING SIGN AND THE PASS-WORD.—The onward sign is the saluting sign in the degree when entering an open Temple. The pass-word is DALMON.

This word will admit you into a Temple that is opened in the Second Degree. If you are present at the opening of the Temple, this is the pass-word you give to prove that you are a Knight of Dalmon.

CLOTHING.—I take pleasure in presenting to you the regalia of a Knight of Dalmon. The Chief Drill Master will place them in proper form upon you. Please notice the color is scarlet, trimmed with white lace. These colors were worn by the Knights of Dalmon of ancient days, as a distinguishing mark of their fidelity to each other. They were called Brothers of Dalmon. This Order existed in Assyria for many years. They were noted lovers of their country, and the most trusted defenders of the empire in time of war. Death had no terrors for them. They believed in the immortality of the soul. The mystic bonds that held them together were never broken, each link in their chain of friendship was welded together by Love and Truth. We trust you, and enroll you as one of the Dalmon Band.

I present to you this javelin with its iron point. It will remind you of the iron-like strength of the Order of Twelve, and tells you when in the fiery furnace of trouble you become more firmly welded to the endless chain of locks.

C. M. gives three raps, all stand. I now announce that Mr. H. A. has received the Dalmon Lock with full instructions. Sir D. M., you will please seat Sir H. A. in his proper place as a Knight of Dalmon.

If there is no further business, the Temple is closed in the same form as in the First Degree, except that the signs used are the Dalmon signs.

The following lecture, or some part of it, must be given before the Temple is closed.

LECTURE, SECOND DEGREE.

Q. Did you ever return to the Mount?
A. I did, by a secret way.
Q. How is that way guarded?
A. It is guarded by the endless lock.
Q. Why is it called endless?
A. Because this lock forms a perfect chain.
Q. Where were you prepared to receive that lock?

A. I was prepared in the threshing floor of Ornan, the Jebusite.

Q. You have traveled, then?

A. Yes; I have traveled from the Mount to the porch of the Temple.

Q. Did you meet any obstructions?

A. I did, at the inner gate.

Q. What was said to you there?

A. Who are you, and why are you here?

Q. What was your answer?

A. A Brother Knight, who desires to be introduced in true Knighthood.

Q. By what means did you get this far on your journey?

A. I rode well, stood well, squared well, and passed the Temple of Knights.

Q. What greeting do you bring to tell of the past?

A. That which I received when I passed the Temple.

Q. Can you give them to me?

A. I will, with your assistance.   (They here give the grip and word.)

Q. What was said to you then?

A. Come in, thou blessed of the Lord, stranger nor foe art thou; we welcome thee with warm accord, our Friend and Brother.

Q. Who was called to witness your vow?

A. Men and angels.

Q. What was further done with you?

A. I was stood at the Temple House, my right hand on the Holy Bible, my left hand on my heart.   In that position I took a solemn obligation that made me a Knight of Dalmon Lock.

Q. How were you disposed of?

A. I was made to see light, having been in darkness.

Q. What did you receive?

A. I was instructed in the secret language of the Lock Degree.

Q. Have you the pass?

A. I have.

Q. Will you divide it with me?

A. I will, if you will begin.

Q. I will give my part of the good name: DAL.

A. My answer makes the full pass: DALMON.

THE THIRD,

—OR—

KEY KNIGHT'S DEGREE.

FORM OF OPENING.

At the proper hour the C. M. takes his seat and gives one rap. This calls the Knights to order, and the officers and members to their seats.

C. M.—Sir Knights, we are preparing to open.......... Temple, No.... If there are any persons present that are not members of this degree, or the Order, I will thank them to retire.

C. M. gives one rap. The C. D. M. advances to the Chief.

The Chief says: Sir D. M., you will please to attend, and receive the word and report.

C. D. M. to C. M.—Sir Chief, I have visited all, and find each person in full possession of the Pass.

C. M.—It is well. Sir D. M., you will please to place the C. St. at his post and invest him; inform him that we are ready to open........... Temple, No...., and order him to let none enter or pass out until further order from the Chief.

The C. D. M. places the C. St. outside of the door with instructions, closes the door and gives three raps; this is answered by the C. St. by three raps; C. D. M. gives one and C. St. answers by one.

The C. D. M. returns to the C. M. and says: Sir Chief, the C. St. is at his post with full instructions.

C. M.—It is well. Let us prepare in the regular form. (The officers, members and visitors put on their regalia.) The C. M. gives two raps, and officers stand.

C. M.—Sir C. D. M., your duty in and about the Temple?

C. D. M.—My duty is to take charge of the inner door, to

27

see that none pass or re-pass without permission from the Chief.

C. M. to C. D. M.—The C. St.'s post and duty?

C. D. M.—His post is at the outer door; his duty is to keep off all who are not members, and take charge of and prepare the rooms for meetings.

C. M. to Sir C. G.—Your duty?

First Guard answers: Our duties are to assist the C. M. in giving degrees and preserve decorum during the hours of business.

C. M.—Sir C. T., your duty?

C. T.—My duty is to receive all money and money orders, pay all orders properly drawn, and have my books and papers always ready for inspection.

C. M.—Sir C. S., your duty?

C. S.—My duty is to keep a record of the doings of the Temple, collect all dues and other money belonging to the Temple, pay the same to the C. T., report quarterly to the Grand Chief and Temple, and annually to the Grand Session.

C. M.—Sir V.-M., your duty?

V.-M.—My duty is to assist the C. M. in his presence, and in his absence perform all his duties.

C. M.—Sir V.-M., the C. M.'s duty?

V.-M.—His duty is to preside at all meetings of the Temple, call special meetings when business requires it, decide all questions of rules and regulations, see that the By-Laws of his Temple and the Edicts of the Grand Temple and C. G. M. are strictly enforced, and represent his Temple at the Grand Session.

C. M.—Sir C. O., your duty? (Gives three raps, all stand.)

C. O.—My duty is to conduct the devotional exercises of the Temple, visit and give consolation to the sick, and attend to the funeral services of Sir Knights and Daughters.

C. M.—Sir Knights, assemble in form. (They assemble on the square, face in.)

C. M.—Sir Knights, to the right-about face, deposit swords, doff caps, left-about face, to your devotions.

The C. O. conducts, as follows:

GOD'S GOODNESS.

Come, let us join our Lord to praise,
  Whose mercy knows no end;
To Him our cheerful voices raise,
  Our Father and our Friend.

In tender infancy, His care
  Preserved our lives from harm;
And now He keeps us from the snare
  Of sin's deceitful charm.

PRAYER.

O, Almighty God, who has built Thy temple upon the foundation of Thy almighty power and word. The Messiah himself being the chief head of the corner-stone, the rock and key-stone of our faith. Grant that we may be so joined together in the unity of spirit by the teachings, that we may be made an Holy Temple acceptable unto Thee, our Lord and Savior. Amen! Amen!! Amen!!!

C. M.—Sir Knights, right-about face, recover swords, cover heads, to the left-about face, march to seats and stand.

C. M.—Sir Knights, assist me in the signs. (In the Third Degree all the signs are given.)

C. M.—We now proclaim............Temple, No...., open in the Third Degree, in Friendship, Love and Harmony.

C. M.—Sir D. M., you will notify the C. St. that...... Temple, No...., is now open, and if there are any members of the Third Degree that wish to enter, admit them by the inner door, provided they are properly clothed and have the pass.

BUSINESS.

The Temple has met to give the degree.

KEY KNIGHT'S DEGREE.

C. M.—I have been informed that Brother.............is waiting in the preparation room to receive the Key Knight's Degree. Sir D. M., you, with the assistance of the Chief Guards, prepare the candidate in regular form to receive the Key Knight's Degree.

The D. M. prepares the Brother by blindfolding, and returns and takes his seat.

The C. G. gives three loud raps.

C. D. M. rises and says: Sir Chief, our Temple is assembled in Harmony for work, we hear an unusual loud call at our door.

C. M.—You will please answer the call and report the cause.

C. D. M. goes to the door and gives three loud raps, opens the door and says: Who is this that disturbs the Harmony of our Temple?

C. G.—A Brother Knight who has the Title and the Lock, and is now in search of the Key.

C. D. M.—What recommendations does he bring?

C. G.—Greetings from Brother Knights of the Lock, and from the porch of the Temple.

C. D. M.—What word do you report from the Lock, what greeting from the porch?

C. G.—I have been taught to STAND TRUE to a Brother Knight; these are my greetings.

C. D. M.—You are right. I will inform the C. M. of your request, and return you his answer.

The C. D. M. closes the door, approaches the C. M., gives three raps, which is answered by the C. M., who asks the same questions and answers returned at the inner door.

C. M.—Let him enter, and commence his pilgrimage in search of the Key. C. D. M. returns to the door and opens it and says: Brother Knight, enter and commence your pilgrimage in search of the Key.

When they enter, the C. M. gives three raps, and all stand. As the D. M. and Brother pass around three times, the following is read by the C. O.

TIME IS FLYING.

How long sometimes a day appears,
  And weeks, how long are they?
Months move along as if the years
  Would never pass away.

But months and years are passing by
  And soon must all be gone;
For day by day, as minutes fly,
  Eternity comes on.

Days, months and years must have an end;
  Eternity has none;
'Twill always have as long to spend
  As when it first begun.

Great God, an infant cannot tell
  How such a thing can be;
I only pray that I may dwell
  That long, long time with Thee.

As the reading is ended, the D. M. and candidate are in the centre of the hall with the Chief Orator, and the other Knights form a circle around the three with hands linked together.

D. M.—My Brother, you have a dangerous road to travel. Before you start, let us kneel and pray. The C. O. prays slowly and solemnly:

PRAYER.

O, God, whose mercy is everlasting and power infinite, look down with pity and compassion upon the sufferings of this, Thy servant: and whether Thou visitest for trial of his patience or punishment of his offenses, enable him by Thy grace cheerfully to submit himself to Thy holy will and pleasure. Go not far from those, O Lord, whom Thou hast laid in a place of darkness, and in the deep; and forasmuch as Thou hast not cut him off suddenly, but chasteneth him as a father, grant that he, duly considering Thy great mercies, may be unfeignedly thankful, and turn unto Thee with true repentance and sincerity of heart, through Jesus Christ, our Lord. Amen! Amen!! Amen!!!

777.—After prayer the Chief Guards lift him up and carry him to the preparation room and tie him to the cooler (a large arm-chair), the Guards carry him around the hall once in a swinging motion; they rest the cooler at the first 777.

C. M.—(To Brother Knight.)—You are now upon the first entrance. Before going further you must answer this question: Do you promise to protect and defend a Knight of Phyletus? The Brother Knight answers (prompted by the C. G.): I will, in every time of need.

333.—The Brother is carried to the next square.

C. M.—Will you befriend and aid a poor, distressed Daughter of the Tabernacle by your means and otherwise? The Brother answers (prompted): I will, freely, as my ability will permit.

999.—The Brother is carried to the third square.

C. M.—Will you risk your life to save a Knight from death when he gives the Grand Sign of Distress or utters the Distress Word? The Brother answers (prompted): I will, and use all the strength I have.

444.—The Brother is carried to the fourth square.

C. M. says: Will you keep the secrets of the Temple and the Tabernacle, and those of a Sir Knight and Daughter, when given to you? The Brother answers: I will, with all my mind, with all my heart, and with all my will.

C. M.—You have said well. Sir C. G's, convey the Brother to the Vice-Mentor for examination. He is swung around the hall once, and stops at the V.-M's station.

C. G.—Sir Vice, we are ordered to report to you for examination.

V.-M.—Who are you that desire my permission to pass this road to the resting place of the Knights of Phyletus?

C. G.—We are Brother Knights, and have opened the first, second, third and fourth entrances. We promise to DEFEND, AID, OBEY, and be SILENT.

V.-M.—It is well done. Unbind our Brother and conduct him to the Chief Mentor, and inform him that this Brother Knight is prepared to receive the Key. (The C. G. and Brother march slowly around the hall, while the following is sung in a low voice):

THE GOODNESS OF GOD.

How kind in all His works and ways
  Must our Creator be;
We learn some lessons of His praise
  From everything we see.
The glorious sun that blazes high,
  The moon more pale and dim,
With all the stars that fill the sky,
  Are made and ruled by Him.
And this vast world of ours below,
  The water and the land,
And all the trees and flowers that grow,
  Were fashioned by His hand.

(At the ending of the last verse the C. G. and Brother stop at the C. M's station.)

C. G.—Sir Chief, the Vice-Mentor sends this Brother to you with greetings, and he said to me to inform you that he was prepared to receive the Key.

C. M.—Thank you. Conduct him to the Temple House, and place him in proper position to take the obligation of a Key Knight. (He kneels on both knees, with his left hand on the Bible, open at the sixth chapter of First Kings, in his right hand a sword.)

C. G.—Sir Chief, the Brother Knight is in proper form to take the obligation of a Key Knight.

C. M.—Thank you. (He gives three raps, and all the Knights form a hollow square around the Chief Orator, Chief Guards and Brother Knight.)

C. O.—Brother Knight, you are now in position to take upon yourself the obligation of a Key Knight. You will please repeat your full name, and say after me:

OBLIGATION.

I, ..., in presence of the Supreme Ruler of the Universe, and these Key Knights, do most solemnly and sincerely promise and swear, in addition to my former obligations, that I will keep and conceal the secrets of this degree, and will not reveal them to a Brother Knight of the lesser degrees, except to assist in making him a Key Knight—nor to any person in the known world.

I further promise that I will obey the Constitution, Rules and Regulations and Edicts of the Grand Temple and Tabernacle; and the National Grand Temple and Tabernacle; the Constitution, Rules and By-Laws of this Temple, or of any other of which I may hereafter become a member.

I further promise that I will obey the Grand Sign of Distress, and go to the relief of the person that gives it. Should it be dark, and the sign cannot be seen, I will obey the hailing figure.

I further promise that I will not confer the Temple Degrees on a woman, an atheist, a fool, or madman.

I further promise that I will obey all signs of a Sir Knight or Daughter, when and wherever given, and also the Secret Lock.

I further promise that I will defend the good name of a Knight or Daughter at any time or place.

I further promise that I will aid and assist poor and indigent Sir Knights and Daughters—I knowing them to be worthy— when I can do it without injury to myself or family.

I further promise that I will not debauch or violate the virtue of a Sir Knight's wife, sister, daughter or widow, nor permit it to be done, if in my power to prevent it.

I further promise that I will not open and organize a Temple or Tabernacle unless I am legally authorized by the proper authority.

I further promise that if any part of my obligation is omitted at this time, I will hold myself amenable when informed thereof.

All of which I do most solemnly promise to fulfill, binding myself, under no less penalty than to have my bones broken and life crushed out, should I willfully break or violate this, my obligation, as a Key Knight. So help me God to keep the same.

The candidate is made to stand.

Sir Chief.—(To Brother.)—Thus far you have come. What is your desire now?

Brother (prompted): I desire to see the Sir K....ts and learn their friendly art.

Sir Chief.—It shall be as you wish. Sirs, look well and make darkness light. *   *   *

(As the shock is given, the bandage falls from the Brother's eyes.)

Sir Chief gives one rap, and all the Knights are seated, except the C. G. and Brother. The Chief then instructs the newly initiated Brother in the signs, words and grips of the Key Degree; he reminds the Brother of his obligation, and tells him that he is about to be Knighted, and that true Friendship is the only road to perfect happiness.

CALLING SIGN.—The fingers of both hands interlaced, dropped at full length of the arms and drawn up to touch the chin. This sign calls a Key Knight to you from any distance it can be seen.

HAILING SIGN.—This sign is given with the left hand drawn across the mouth. It is the answering sign to the calling sign.

When a Knight receives the calling sign he hails it with the left hand, as above, this tells the Knight who gives the calling sign that you are a Key Knight, and that you are ready for a further test, either by lecture, or the grips and words.

GRAND SIGN OF DISTRESS.—This sign is given by holding the right hand at arm's length above the head, thumb in the palm of the hand, and the four fingers open.

THE GRIP.—(With the touch of detection.)—This grip is given by the common shake of the hand, but with the thumb below the knuckles; this is the first part of the grip. The second part of the grip is to touch the little finger of the one you are shaking hands with; if he is a Knight he will open his little finger and let yours in.

THE GRAND WORD.—U–O–Y–H–T–I–W–M–A–I.
THE ANSWER.—H–T–A–E–D–L–I–T–N–U.
THE PASS-WORD.—S–U–T–E–L–Y–H–P.

This is the word you give when you wish to enter a Temple that is opened in the Key Knight's Degree; it is the pass that is given when opening a Temple in the Third Degree.

THE SECRET LOCK.—**999.**—Are only to be used when you want to send a message to a Knight, to let him know that you demand his presence immediately.

The three nines were sacred numbers, used by the magicians of ancient India in the Pehlvi language, which signifies Priest. The magicians claimed to have the gift of prophecy, and power to control the secret forces of nature. They had for years an unbounded influence over the people. The mysteries of Magnus consist of nine degrees. They used their sacred numbers, 999, to summon members to assemble. If a member, after receiving these, failed to meet, he suffered death, and was seen no more. We use these numbers to summon a Knight. This summons must be obeyed when it is received. Knights are instructed not to use this summons unless the presence of a Knight is absolutely required. It can be used in sickness or distress. The manner of sending this summons is as follows: Write 999, and under the figures your address, and send it by man, woman or child to the Knight you wish to see. If you are a stranger, you can inquire if there is a Temple of the Knights of Tabor; on being informed that there is, tell your messenger to find one of the members, and give the summons to him.

444.—These are only to be used when all other signs fail. They are the grand hailing figures.

Searching the mysteries of Mithra, we find the figure 4 one of their mystic numbers; they worshiped Deity under the name of Agla. The followers of Mithra were numerous and powerful during the time that Phrygia flourished as a kingdom. When necessary for them to assemble, the trumpet was sounded 4–4–4, each four sounded separately and distinctly. It made no difference what the member was doing, everything was abandoned to obey that call. The figures were used when a member was in danger and needed protection. When the 4–4–4 were heard the followers of Mithra never stopped or paused until they found the person that uttered them, and they were prepared to defend him with their lives, or die by his side. You will notice that the name of God was pronounced three distinct times—that is, that the 4–4–4 calls thrice on the Sovereign Ruler of the Universe to witness that you are obeying your obligation. Remember the oath that you have taken.

777.—The figure 7 has in all ages been received as a perfect number. The world we live in was created and made by the Supreme Master Builder of the Universe in seven days. Running all through the pages of Holy Writ we find the symbolized figure 7. The Jews, when they wished to express the divine essence of Deity, used the figure 7. J–E–H–O–V–A–H. In the study of the Odinic rites we find the mysterious triple sevens emblazoned on their banners. When their banners were hoisted and waved, it was a call to assemble, which all obeyed. We use the three sevens (777) as an important emblem. The C. S. of the Temple is required to have the 777 printed in green, and keep them in his office. When these figures are used, all members are required to attend their Temple in a called session, and imperatively demand their presence. The C. S. puts the date and hour on the card, with the 777, and hands or sends it to the member. When a member receives this summons, he must attend. No excuse but sickness can be taken. If he fails to be present at the appointed hour, he violates his obligation, and, on conviction, will be expelled.

333.—When given properly, the order is absolute. The voice that utters it must be found at all hazards.

The mystic figures, 333, the mysterious unity in the Godhead—the Father, the Son, the Holy Spirit—these three are one. The component parts that are found in a human being are three—the Body, the Soul, the Spirit. The three necessaries of life—the Earth, to give us food; the Water, to give us drink; the Air, to give us life. The ancient Druids, when initiating a novice into their mysterious rites, whispered I O W, the name of the Omnipotent and Eternal Power. This symbol of the 3, when repeated three times, the Druids believed would cure all manner of diseases, and was the key that admitted a soul to the land of bliss. The emblematic symbol used in the Ethiopian mysteries was 333, in a triangular form. The first 3 parts which the candidate was required to pass through for purification were *air*, *fire*, and *water*. The second part of the ceremonies was divided into 3 parts. He found himself in a subterranean chamber, overhung with black. He was instructed that black was an emblem of sorrow and trouble, though he had become pure, yet it was the lot of mortals to have sorrow and trouble all the days of their lives. The second chamber was hung with white and black. He was instructed that that was an emblem of the world we live in. The white symbolized *life, health, pleasure* and *happiness*. The black symbolized *life, sickness* and *distress*. The third chamber was hung with pure white. He was instructed that this chamber was an emblem of a mortal that lived a pure life. Now his days are almost ended on earth. Visions of eternal glory fill his thoughts. He sees the luminous 333 on the door of the chamber that he is soon to enter. He hears a sweet, musical voice, saying: "Knock, and it shall open to you." He gives three knocks and repeats in the name of *Elion, Eloi, Noil*. The door silently opens and a voice most thrillingly says: Enter the first step, when he drops the garments of mortality; at the second step he is clothed with the white, glittering robes of immortality; at the third step he is crowned with the jeweled crown of eternity, the heavenly land, his home forever. The scenes that open to his view are beautiful beyond description.

The sublime lessons taught by the symbolized 333, and the cabalistic names of Deity are recommended to your serious and earnest study. We use the 333 in the Daughter of the Tabernacle degrees as the hailing figures of danger and distress. You are instructed, when you hear the hail 333, to not pause or stop until you find the person who gives that hail—you are obligated to save him at the risk of your own life, and to relieve him if in distress. Remember the 333.

C. M. gives three raps, and all Sir Knights assemble on the line. The Chief says: Sir Knights, our Friend and Brother has made a good report of his travels and earned the good title of a Knight of the Lock and Key. You will form the Lock, and we will admit him within the chain.

KNIGHTHOOD.

The Brother kneels on his right knee on the circle "O," with his right hand holding the book, his left hand on his breast.

Sir Chief, with the sword in proper position, says: By the power and authority in me vested, as C. M. of a chartered Temple, I now and here declare C.... B.... a Knight of T. of D. of P. Arise, Sir C.... B...., and fulfill the duties of true Knighthood.

The Sir Knights answer: Amen! Amen!! Amen!!! May the Lord keep him in Union, Friendship and Honor.

The sword is placed in his hand, and he repeats as follows:

"With the hilt of the sword in my hand, and with the point toward an enemy, I promise to defend a Sir Knight, his wife, daughter, sister and widow, until the last enemy is conquered."

C. M.—Attention, Sir Knights. Handle swords, draw swords, present swords, return swords, to the right-about face, march to seats.

C. M. to C. G.—Sir Guards, you will please conduct Sir C. B. to the Chief Orator for further instruction. (The C. M. takes his seat, and the Guards march once around the hall and halt in front of the C. O.

C. G. to C. O.—Sir Orator, the Chief ordered Sir C. B. to appear before you for instruction.

C. O.—Sir Guards, the Chief's orders shall be obeyed. Sir C. B., you have had a long and toilsome journey; many and varied were the scenes you have passed through. You first represented one of the ten thousand armed men of the tribes of Naphtali and Zebulon, who fought and conquered Jabin's host, and freed the captive Israelites. Passing down through several centuries, you again come to the front as a representative of King Solomon's guard of honor, who were most trusted and nearest his person. They were present at the building of the great temple and at its dedication. They were with the king when he received Africa's intelligent and intellectual queen. It was their privilege to listen to the questions and answers of these great monarchs. Solomon was a wise descendant of Shem, and the illustrious queen of Ethiopia, a wise descendant of Ham, traveled hundreds of miles to test the wisdom of Solomon. They met; it was a battle of giant intellects. The queen returned home satisfied that she had met the most learned man living.

You represented the armed warriors that defended Jerusalem when it was captured, and the great temple was destroyed, and the Jews were made captives and carried to Babylon, where they remained for seventy-two years, until Cyrus, king of Persia, restored them to liberty, and ordered them to return to Judea and re-build the temple at Jerusalem. The edict of King Cyrus was not heeded until after his death. When Darius ascended the throne, he confirmed the decree of Cyrus—42,362. The tribes of Judah and Benjamin, under command of Zorobabel, the governor; Joshua, the high priest, and Ezra, the scribe, journeyed from Babylon to Jerusalem. Seven months after the arrival of this host in the ancient city of Jerusalem, the foundation of the second temple was laid with great ceremonies. You, of the Key Knight's Degree, represented the Knights of the Temple. The builders were surrounded by enemies, who tried to stop the workmen. These Knights were compelled to work with their swords girded at their sides, ready for battle.

You have traveled from Mount Tabor to Persia, and there learned the mysteries of Mithra, and received the meaning of true friendship from Dalmon and Phyletus. You have been permitted to lift the veil of the mystic theology of the ancient world. You have had a look at the symbols and rites of the mysteries of Ethiopia, Egypt, Persia, India, Greece, Phoenicia, Assyria, and their cabalistic and mystical mode of explaining the sacred and spiritual work of Deity. You have found the symbolic Lock and Key, but before you can use the symbolized Key effectually and usefully, you must travel further and learn its *ineffable name.*

I present to you this collar and apron. It is worn in this way. Its color is scarlet, ornamented with twelve stars, the color and stars of a Key Knight. I entrust to your care this sword and belt. They are worn in this way. The sword is an emblem of Knighthood. This cap—wear it—it is an emblem of dignity, and of your Knightly position of Tabor, Dalmon and Phyletus. On it is the symbol T. D. P.

C. O. to C. G.—Sir Guards, you will please conduct Sir C. B. to the Chief, and inform him that I have given Sir C. B. full instructions. (They march once around the hall, and stop at the C. M.'s station.)

C. G. to C. M.—Sir Chief, the Chief Orator sends greeting, to tell you that he has fully instructed Sir C. B.

C. M.—Thank you. (He gives three raps, all stand.) Sir Knights, handle swords, draw swords, carry swords, present swords. I now and here declare that Sir C. B. has received the Key Knight's Degree, and is in possession of the Secret Lock and Mystic Key. Sir Knights, salute (they salute three times). Sir Knights, carry swords, return swords. The C. M. gives one rap, and all are seated. He says: Sir Guards, conduct Sir C. B. to a seat.

CLOSING.

C. M.—Sir D. M., we are about to close.........Temple, No...., to stand closed until.........., unless summoned earlier. Please give notice to the C. St.

The C. D. M. gives the notice in proper form, returns and says: Sir Chief, the C. St. is at his post, with full instructions.

C. M.—I thank you. Attention, Sir Knights. (Three raps are given, and all stand.)

C. O. delivers the following (or some other suitable)

PRAYER.

Almighty God, the preserver of all who trust in Thee, we bless Thy great name for the mercies bestowed upon us, and for the harmony vouchsafed to us in our enclosure during this meeting, and as we are now about to disperse, let Thy mercies continue with us, and guide us through life, and in Heaven save us. Amen! Amen!! Amen!!!

The signs are all given.

C. M.—I now declare............Temple, No...., closed until............, in Love, Friendship, Peace and Harmony. (One rap.)

The following lecture, or some part of it, must be repeated before closing:

THIRD DEGREE LECTURE.

Q. Are you a Key Knight?
A. I am; test me.
Q. By what will you be tested?
A. I will be tested by the Secret Key.
Q. Where did you receive that Key?
A. In a regular chartered Temple.
Q. What number constitutes a Temple?
A. The number twelve.
Q. Why do you use the number twelve?
A. Because it is the mystical number of the Order.
Q. How do you apply that number to our Order?
A. Before I could become a perfect Knight, it was necessary that I should be invested with twelve points.
Q. What are the twelve points?
A. 1st, Application; 2d, Recommendation; 3d, Election; 4th, Entrance; 5th, Passing the Squares; 6th, Obligation; 7th, Signs; 8th, Pass-word; 9th, Instruction; 10th, Secret Lock; 11th, Secret Key; 12th, Knighthood.
Q. Where were you prepared to be made a Key Knight?
A. In the cooling room, near a chartered Temple.
Q. How were you prepared?
A. The cooling chair was my bed.
Q. What was then done with you?

A. I was swung around the Temple three times and halted at the first square.

Q. What promise did you make?

A. To defend and protect a Sir Knight whenever and wherever he needs my aid.

Q. What was your second promise?

A. At the second square I promised to befriend and aid a Sir Knight by means or otherwise when in distress.

Q. What will you obey?

A. All calls of the Temple or Tabernacle and of a Sir Knight or Daughter properly given.

Q. What did you promise to keep?

A. The secrets of the Temple and Tabernacle and those of Knights and Daughters given to me.

Q. What was then done with you?

A. I was released, having cleared every square, and conducted to the C. M., where it was declared that we promise to defend, aid, obey, and be silent.

Q. What did the C. M. do with you?

A. I was made to kneel upon my knees and took upon myself the binding oath and obligation of a Key Knight.

Q. What did the C. M. say to you?

A. Thus far have you come, what is your desire now?

Q. What was your answer?

A. I desire to see the Sir Knights and learn their friendly art.

Q. What was there done with you?

A. I was brought from darkness to light.

Q. What instructions did you receive?

A. I was instructed in the signs, words and grips of the Key Degree.

Q. Have you the signs?

A. I have those which were given me.

Q. Will you give them?

A. I will, in this way (signs are here given).

Q. Can you give the grip and word?

A. I will, with your assistance (they are given).

Q. Have you the Secret Lock?

A. I have, and am willing to be tested.

Q. When and where is the Secret Lock to be given?

A. When all other signs fail, and in any place.

Q. By whose authority were you Knighted?

A. By the authority of the C. M. of a chartered Temple.

Q. How were you taught to use the sword?

A. I was taught to grasp the hilt, and hold the point towards an enemy, and, therefore, defend a Sir Knight, his wife, mother, daughter or sister.

THE UNIFORM RANK,

—O R—

FOURTH DEGREE.

THE OFFICERS.

Chief Mentor, C. M.	Chief Drill Master, C. D. M.
Vice-Mentor, V.-M.	Chief Standard Bearer, C. S. B.
Chief Scribe, C. S.	Chief Guard, C. G.
Assistant Scribe, A. S.	Chief Guard, C. G.
Chief Treasurer, C. T.	Chief Guard, C. G.
Chief Orator, C. O.	Chief Sentinel, C. St.

FULL DRESS UNIFORM.—(For public turn-outs.)— Black coat, single breasted, buttoned up in front; buttons of yellow metal, with letters U. K. T.; black pants; helmet, trimmed with gold lace; a shield of yellow metal, with letters U. K. T.; a scarlet feather (C. M. and Past C. M.'s, green feather); a baldric four inches wide; colors, black in the centre and scarlet on each side, trimmed with half inch gold lace; letters, on the left breast, U. K. T., made of yellow metal, the shape of a twelve-pointed star; on the shoulder, three sevens—777—(C. M. and past C. M.'s, colors black and green); where the ends of the baldric cross, a seven-pointed star, with letters U. K. T. All metal used on the baldric is yellow. Gauntlets same color as baldric, made to reach from wrist half way to elbow, trimmed with gold lace, and letters U. K. T.; gloves of yellow lisle thread; sword and silver scabbard, shield on hilt lettered U. K. T.; scarlet belt; silver chains, with hooks for cup and cap; the cap trimmed with silver lace and lettered U. K. T.; C. M. and past C. M.'s, yellow metal for scabbard, chains, lace and letters.

UNDRESS UNIFORM.—When giving the degree, or on fatigue duty, the undress uniform is a cap, sword, belt and gloves.

THE HALL.—Hanging over the C. M.'s post is a small black and green banner, with the letters U. K. T. in the centre. Over the V.-M.'s post is a black and scarlet banner, with the letters U. K. T. The curtains at the windows are black and scarlet. The C. M.'s pedestal is covered with a green cloth. The V.-M.'s pedestal is covered with a scarlet cloth. The Temple House is covered with a black cloth. The altar is covered with a pure white cloth. On it, when giving a degree, is a Bible, opened at Judges, 4th chapter, and on it a sword without a scabbard, its hilt toward the C. M. Around the altar is a hollow square, formed thus:

```
333                    777



           O

       O   Altar.

           O



999                    444
```

OPENING.

Not less than twelve Uniform Knights must be present at the opening.

The C. M. takes his post and gives one rap, for attention, and then a second rap, and every officer takes his post. A third rap calls the attention of the Drill Master.

C. M.—Sir Drill Master, please draw near to the Chief and receive the pass. The Drill Master goes direct to the C. M. and receives the pass in a whisper—*Calanthe.*

C. M.—You will please visit all that are present and receive the pass. If there are any present who have not the pass, conduct them to the ante-room. (The Drill Master visits all, and those not having the pass are conducted to the ante-room; then returns to his post.)

D. M. to C. M.—Sir Chief, all that are in the hall are Uniform Knights of Tabor.

C. M.—I thank you, Sir Drill Master. You will please place the Chief Sentinel on duty at his post, and instruct him to admit no person until further orders from the Chief. (The Drill Master attends to the Chief's orders and returns to his post.)

D. M. to C. M.—Sir Chief, I have fulfilled your orders; the Chief Sentinel is at his post of duty, obeying your instructions.

C. M.—I thank you. Sir Knights, prepare for duty. (At this command the Knights put on their undress uniform and are seated at their several posts.)

C. M. gives three raps, all the officers stand. (If any officer is not present, the C. M. orders a Knight to fill the post *pro-tem.*)

C. M. to D. M.—Sir Drill Master, where are you, and what are your duties?

D. M. to C. M.—Sir Chief, I am at my post. My duties are to guard the inner entrance of Mount Tabor, and admit none except ordered by the Chief, and to command the Knights when they are under marching orders.

C. M.—I thank you. Where is the Chief Sentinel, and what are his duties?

D. M. to C. M.—The Chief Sentinel is on duty at the outer entrance. He is there with instructions to guard the entrance, and to admit none but by order of the Chief, and to see that all are properly clothed before they enter this plateau.

C. M.—I thank you. Where are the Chief Guards?

D. M. to C. M.—They are at their posts in the plateau, between the centre and the outer lines.

C. M. to C. G.'s—What are your duties, Sir Guards?

C. G.'s to C. M.—(Only one of the Guards answers.)—Sir

Chief, it is our duty to assist the Chief in keeping order on the plateau, when it is open for work, and to inspect the candidates, prepare them for their reception, and assist in their initiation.

C. M. to C. G.—I thank you. Where is the Chief Banner Bearer?

C. G. to C. M.—He is at his post, to the left of the plateau, between the centre and the inner lines.

C. M. to C. B. B.—What are your duties, Sir Banner Bearer?

C. B. B. to C. M.—Sir Chief, it is my duty to guard the banner of Mount Tabor, and to unfurl it when the Knights are under marching orders, and to defend it when in battle.

C. M. to C. B. B.—Thank you. Where is the Chief Scribe?

C. B. B. to C. M.—He is at his post, to the left of the inner lines of the plateau.

C. M. to C. S.—Sir Scribe, what are your duties?

C. S. to C. M.—Sir Chief, my duties are to make and keep a roll of the members, to record the business of Mount Tabor, and, by order of the Chief, to issue all notices and summons.

C. M. to C. S.—I thank you. Where is the Chief Treasurer?

C. S. to C. M.—He is at his post, to the right of the inner lines of the plateau.

C. M. to C. T.—Sir Treasurer, what are your duties?

C. T. to C. M.—Sir Chief, it is my duty to be present at every meeting on Mount Tabor, and to receive from the Chief Scribe the money he has collected from the Uniform Knights, and to give him my receipt therefor, also, to pay all warrants drawn on the Treasurer, when they are signed by the Chief and countersigned by the Chief Scribe, and to account for all money that I receive and pay out, and be ready to report, at any meeting, the condition of the treasury.

C. M. to C. T.—Thank you. Where is the Chief Orator?

C. T. to C. M.—He is at his post, to the right of the centre of the plateau.

C. M. to C. O.—Sir Orator, what are your duties?

C. O. to C. M.—Sir Chief, it is my duty to attend to the devotional exercises on Mount Tabor, to visit sick members and give consolation when needed, and to assist in the funeral ceremonies.

C. M. to C. O.—Thank you. Where is the Vice-Mentor?

C. O. to C. M.—He is at his post, in the outer centre of the plateau.

C. M. to V.-M.—Sir Vice, what are your duties?

V.-M. to C. M.—Sir Chief, my duties are to be present at all meetings on Mount Tabor, to assist the Chief in conducting the business in the plateau, and to preside when the Chief is absent.

C. M. to V.-M.—I thank you. Where is the Chief, and what are his duties?

V.-M. to C. M.—The Chief is at his post, in the inner centre of the plateau. His duties are to preside at all meetings on Mount Tabor, to issue commands, to call meetings, and to assemble the Knights for business. He is, to govern fairly, justly and impartially, and to obligate candidates, and instruct them, assisted by the officers in the plateau.

C. M. to V.-M.—I thank you. Sir Drill Master, please assemble the Knights on the centre square for devotion.

C. D. to Knights.—Sir Knights, attention! Mark time, forward march. (The Knights, from their several places in the plateau march direct to the centre square, and form a hollow square around the altar, the C. O. standing on the "O" at the right side of the altar, the D. M. on 999, the V.-M. on 444, the C. S. on 777, and the C. T. on 333.)

C. D. to C. M.—Sir Chief, the Knights are waiting for your commands.

The D. M. conducts the C. M. to the "O" in front of the

altar. (The centre square must be large enough for all the Knights to stand, with their toes on the line.)

C. M. to Knights.—Sir Knights, attention! To the right-about face, deposit caps. To the left-about face, handle swords, draw swords, present swords, deposit swords. (All lay down their swords, pointing to the altar.) Sir Knights, let us offer our prayers to God, the Supreme Governor of the Universe. (All kneel on their right knee, arms across the breast.)

The C. O. offers the following, or another appropriate prayer:

PRAYER.

Oh Lord, our Heavenly Father, we come at this hour, confessing our many sins, asking that Thou, who art wonderful and all-merciful in Thy dealings with mankind, look upon Thy servants bowed here, and in pity forgive our many sins of commission and omission. We pray that Thou bless every Knight of Tabor and their families with an outpouring of Thy love and mercy. Teach us to measure our days, give us strength to do Thy will, bind us together in the cords of Friendship everlasting. When the Golden Bowl is broken, and the sleep of death comes to us, Oh Lord, in the dissolution that frees the soul, be Thou our Guide to the Heavenly Temple of Eternal Rest, and we will give Thee all glory and honor throughout endless ages. Amen! Amen!! Amen!!!

All the Knights say: Holy is the Lord, God, praise His name.

C. M. to Knights.—Arise, Sir Knights, and form the Cord of Friendship. (This is done by locking arms and clasping the right and left hands together, fingers interlaced.)

C. M.—May the Cord of Friendship in this plateau never be broken.

All the Knights answer: We will be as Dalmon and Phyletus—true to the end.

C. M.—Sir Knights, locked as we are, let me try the Test of Friendship, let us pass the test around.

(The C. M. whispers the test to the Knight on his left, one

whispers it to another, until it gets back to the C. M. If it comes right, the C. M. says: The test is true. If it does not come up right, they try it again, until all have it—*Dionysius.*)

C. M. to Knights.—Recover swords, present swords, return swords, to the right-about face, recover caps, forward march to post of duty. (All go to their places.)

C. M. gives four distinct raps and says: I proclaim this plateau open for work, drill, or business. (He then gives one rap, when all are seated.)

C. M. to C. O.—Sir Orator, you will please prepare the altar. (The C. O. opens the Bible at Judges, 4th chapter, and places on it a sword, without a scabbard, its hilt toward the C. M.

C. M. to D. M.—Sir Drill Master, please notify the Chief Sentinel that our plateau is open. If there is any Knight that is a visitor or member of this plateau who wishes to enter, please report his name. (The D. M. gives two raps on the portal, this is answered by the C. St. giving two raps. The D. M. gives two more raps, the C. St. answers by two raps and opens the wicket. The D. M. whispers the C. M.'s orders and gives the raps, the C. St. answers by the same.)

C. D. to C. M.—Sir Chief, the Chief Sentinel is on duty at his post.

C. M. to C. D.—I thank you.

C. D. to C. M.—Sir Chief, I hear the tocsin. (The tocsin is an alarm bell rung by the C. St. to notify the C. D. that he is wanted at the portal.)

C. M. to C. D.—Sir Drill Master, attend the call of the tocsin. (The C. D. gives the raps at the portal and is answered by the C. St., he then opens the wicket and informs the C. D. that Sir K. L. is prepared to enter, but cannot give the pass.)

C. D. to V.-M.—Sir Vice, Sir K. L. is prepared to enter; and Sir B. K. desires to enter, but cannot give the pass.

V.-M. to C. D.—Sir Drill Master, let Sir K. L. enter. (A

Knight that enters the plateau must advance behind the altar with drawn sword, stand on the "O" and salute the C. M., and turn to the left and salute the V.-M., and take his seat.)

V.-M. to Knights.—Sir Knights, Sir B. K. desires to enter, but cannot give the pass, is he known to the plateau? If there is a Knight present who knows Sir B. K. belongs to the rank of any plateau, he rises and says: Sir B. K. is a member of the plateau. (A Knight cannot give this assurance if he has not met the applying Knight in an open plateau. If the applicant is not known to any of the rank, the C. M. appoints a committee of three to examine him. On their report he is admitted or requested to retire from Mount Tabor.)

V.-M. to C. D.—Sir Drill Master, you are authorized to give Sir B. K. the pass, and tell the C. St. to let him enter.

C. M. to C. S.—Sir Scribe, have you anything at your post requiring the attention of the plateau?

C. S. to C. M.—Sir Chief, on my desk is the petition of H. A. I also notified Sir O. W. to be present at this meeting to receive the degree. I suppose he is in the reception room.

C. M. to C. S.—Sir Scribe, please read the petition, we will act on that first, and give the degree next, if the candidate is present.

The C. S. reads:

PETITION.

To the members of................Temple, No.... The undersigned, believing the Knights of Tabor a good institution, wishes to become a member, and asks to be accepted. Age........., Residence........., Occupation........., Enclosed fee $......, Recommended by.................
Dated.............A. D., 18..
           Signed...........................Petitioner.

The C. M. orders the Guards to prepare the ballot box— which is done by putting the white and black balls in one apartment—and to set the box on the altar. The A. S. calls the roll, and the members vote when their names are called.

(The white balls cast elect the candidate, and the black balls reject him. If four black balls are found among those cast, he is rejected, and can make application again after three months. If there be a mistake made, in the opinion of the C. M., he can order another ballot to be taken immediately.)

When all have voted, the C. M. orders the Guards to count the ballots, and pass the box to the V.-M., who looks into the box, and requests the Guards to take it to the C. M. The C. M. examines the ballots and gives four raps, all stand, when he says: I proclaim that Sir H. A. is elected to receive the full degrees of the Temple and plateau. Sir Scribe, you will please notify him to that effect. (If the C. M. finds that the candidate is not elected, he so announces.) The C. M. gives one rap, and the members are seated.

C. M. to D. M.—Sir Drill Master, please inquire at the portal if Sir O. W. is present. (The D. M. gives the usual raps, and receives the same from the C. St., who opens the wicket and answers that the candidate is in the preparation room.)

D. M. to C. M.—Sir Chief, your orders have been obeyed. (The C. St. reports that the candidate is in the preparation room. Not more than four candidates can be initiated at one meeting, except in organizing, and then not more nor less than twelve. The plateau can meet to initiate members as often as needed, and may ballot for members at every meeting.)

C. M. to D. M.—I thank you. Sir Guards, you will please prepare the candidate. (The Guards go from the plateau into the preparation room direct.)

One of the Guards to candidate.—We have come to investigate. If you do not pass our examination, you must retire from Mount Tabor.

QUESTIONS.

1. How old are you?
2. How long have you been a member of the Order of Twelve?

3. How long have you been a Key Knight?
4. Have you full use of your right hand?
5. Can you kneel on your right knee?
6. Can you walk without limping?
7. Are you temperate in your habits?
8. Are you married?
9. Do you believe in God?
10. Do you believe in future reward and punishment, as spoken of in the Holy Bible?
11. If you take an oath in the name of God, can you violate or break that oath?
12. Would you be willing to die rather than break an oath taken before God and man?
13. Will you, if you are admitted a member of this plateau, continue and remain a firm friend to every member of the Uniform Rank?
14. Will you continue to live a respectable life and be an honorable citizen?

(These questions must be written, or printed copies kept in the plateau. The answers must be written opposite the questions.)

One of the Guards returns to the plateau with the questions and answers, and stands at the altar.

C. G. to C. M.—Sir Chief, we have investigated the candidate, and have here the answers.

C. M. to C. G.—Sir Guard, you will please give the investigation to the Chief Scribe. (The C. S. reads aloud, slowly and distinctly.) The C. M. gives four raps, all stand.

C. M. to Knights.—Sir Knights, you have heard the answers in the investigation; are you satisfied?

All answer, *we are.* (If there is one who says he is not satisfied, he must prove, by two or more members, that the candidate is not a reliable man; if it is so proven, the candidate is rejected, and he must retire from Mount Tabor.)

The C. M. gives one rap, and all are seated.

THE DEGREE.

The candidate is prepared as follows: Both arms are tied

close to his sides by a rope around his body; a red bag, made of heavy cotton, is made to cover his head, and hang below his shoulders. (The cotton must be thick enough so that he cannot see through it. Three or four bags must be kept in the plateau, so as to accommodate all candidates.)

The Guards march the candidate into the plateau in silence. They slowly march four times around the plateau, keeping the altar on the right. They halt at the V.-M.'s post.

One of the Guards to V.-M.—Sir Vice, you see before you a Key Knight, who has successfully been invested with the twelve points of Taborian Knighthood, and is ready, having made every preparation to receive the Fourth Degree, or Uniform Rank.

V.-M. to C. G.—Sir Guard, you say he has been invested with the twelve points of Taborian Knighthood?

V.-M. to Candidate.—Will you name the points?

Candidate to V.-M.—Sir Vice, the 1st point is Application; the 2d, Recommendation; the 3d, Election; the 4th, Entrance; the 5th, Passing the Squares; the 6th, Obligation; the 7th, Signs; the 8th, Pass-word; the 9th, Instruction; the 10th, Secret Lock; the 11th, Secret Key; the 12th, Knighthood. (The Guards may find it necessary to prompt the candidate in his answers.)

V.-M. to Candidate.—You have proved that you are a perfect Knight of Tabor, Dalmon and Phyletus. You are now at the outer centre of the plateau, on Mount Tabor. You are about to learn the deep, untold mysteries of Mount Tabor. They who enter the inner centre of Mount Tabor must have courage, and a firm determination to be true to every member of the plateau. You will not be permitted to violate an obligation and live. The seven tests of true, firm friendship will be unfolded to you. If you fail in any one of these tests, you will never see another sunrise. Consider well before you go further. If your conscience tells you that you are a true man, I advise you to go forward. If you feel that you cannot conform to the secret tests, my advice is that you retire, and go no further on the plateau.

After waiting a minute or two, the V.-M. asks: What have you decided on?

Candidate to V.-M.—(Prompted by the Guards.)—I will go forward to the inner centre.

V.-M. to C. G.—Sir Guards, you are authorized to conduct this Key Knight into the inner centre. When you arrive at the post of the inner Guard, he will demand of you the inner pass. Give him this with your sword's point resting on the floor of the plateau—*Zebulon*. (They march once around the plateau, and halt opposite the C. D. M.'s post.)

C. D. M.—Halt! Who are you that approaches the inner centre?

C. G.—(Resting the points of swords on the floor.)—There are two tribes. We are of *Zebulon*.

C. D. M.—(Resting the point of his sword on the floor.)— We have been looking for you, enter in the name of *Naphtali*. (The C. D. M. and C. G.'s salute and return swords.)

C. D. M.—My orders, received from Barak, are, that when Zebulon came, to admit him and conduct him to the Chief Orator. (The C. G.'s conduct the candidate once around the plateau, and halt at the C. O.'s post.)

C. G. to C. O.—Sir Chief Orator, I was ordered to conduct this Key Knight to your post by the C. D. M., and to inform you that he is prepared to receive the seven tests.

C. O. to Candidate.—You have come this far; the next step will open the full plateau to you, and you will be enrolled a member, if you are permitted to pass this post. You will please place your open right hand on the open Holy Bible. (The Bible lays in front of the C. O., opened at the 4th chapter of Judges.) You are now in proper position to take the seven tests. I warn you to answer, without mental reservation. Your life depends upon your answers.

THE TESTS.

C. O.—1st. Do you believe in God, the Supreme Ruler and Governor of Mankind?

Candidate.—I firmly believe in God, and that he has full power to reward those who obey and believe in Him, and that He has power to punish those who disobey His commands.

C. O.—2d. Are you satisfied that there is a Heaven for the good and just, and a hell for the bad and unjust, who die without repentance?

Candidate.—I am fully convinced that there is a Heaven for the good and just, and a hell for the bad and unjust, who die without repentance.

C. O.—3d. Do you believe that an obligation taken in the name of God is binding as long as you have life in your body?

Candidate.—I sincerely believe that an obligation, taken in the sacred name of God, binds me to what I promise as long as I live.

C. O.—4th. You are about to be obligated a member of this plateau; will you promise never to reveal its secrets to mortal man, except when you are giving the degree, or assisting in giving it, or for instruction to members?

Candidate.—I will remember my obligation, and carefully keep my promise and secret oath.

C. O.—5th. Do you promise never to impart the secrets of a Uniform Knight of Tabor to woman, either by word or sign, or in any other manner, so as to enable her to guess at any part of the secrets?

Candidate.—I promise to be guarded in the presence of women, and never reveal to them the secrets of a Uniform Knight by word or act.

C. O.—6th. Many persons become members of an Order, belong to it for a longer or shorter time, and are by some unavoidable circumstance *suspended* or *expelled*—a true Knight is never suspended or expelled, unless through unavoidable causes. If you should be so unfortunate as to have the sentence of suspension or expulsion passed upon you, will you even then keep your lips sealed, and not expose the secrets that you have learned on the plateau?

Candidate.—I will never, under any circumstances, willfully and knowingly expose the secrets of the Uniform Knighthood.

C. O.—7th. When initiated as a Key Knight, you were told that the work was finished when the Key fits the Lock. The explanation was not given to you. Do you promise to obey the teachings of the mysterious Key?

Candidate.—I received the Secret Lock, and was informed that the Key was fitted to the Lock, but I received no further explanation. I will obey the teachings of the mysterious Key, when I receive it.

(Let the candidate give the answers in his own words. If not satisfactorily given, prompt him in giving the true answers.)

C. O. to C. G.'s—Sir Chief Guards, you are hereby requested to conduct the candidate to the central altar, and place him in proper position, and inform the Chief Mentor that the candidate has passed the seven tests and is within the hollow square, in proper position to be received as a member of the plateau.

(The C. G.'s conduct the candidate once around the plateau, slowly and in silence, and stand him at the altar with his face toward the C. M., then one of the C. G.'s marches to the post of the inner centre, and salutes the C. M. with his sword.)

C. G. to C. M.—Sir Chief, I am requested by the Chief Orator to inform you that the candidate has passed the seven tests and is now at the central altar, ready to receive your orders.

C. M. to C. G.—Sir Guard, I am pleased to hear that *Zebulon* has arrived and is ready to be enrolled with *Naphtali;* you are ordered to take your proper place within the square.

(The C. G. salutes the Chief and marches to his proper place.

The **Chief** gives four distinct **raps**, and all **stand**; he then silently takes his place at the altar, the C. O. to his right and the Guards immediately behind the candidate. The Chief waves his left hand and the Knights form silently around the square, with their toes resting on the lines. The Chief waves a second time, and the Knights silently draw their swords and point them toward the candidate. The Chief takes the hilt of the sword that lays on the Bible in his right hand and lets the point rest on the open Bible. The Chief waves his left hand, and the Guards lift the veil from the candidate's head.)

C. M. to Candidate.—You are here, in the centre of the plateau of Mount Tabor. Around you are your friends, who will, with drawn swords, defend you when in danger. Before you can demand their full aid and protection, you must receive an obligation that will bind Zebulon to Naphtali as long as life shall last. It is the bond of friendship, the union of hearts, and unity of action. You will please kneel on your right knee, and place your right hand on the open Bible, palm downward, and repeat after me:

The Guards lay the points of their swords on the candidate's right shoulder. (If there are more candidates than Guards, other Knights assist.) The Knights on the lines rest the points of their swords on the floor of the plateau. The three candles are lighted on the Temple House, and all the working tools are placed on or around the Temple House.

THE OBLIGATION.

I, ..., in the presence of God, the Father; God, the Son, and God, the Holy Ghost, in the name of the Holy Trinity, do hereby swear (or affirm) that I will remember and fulfill my answers given in the seven secret tests. I further swear (or affirm) that I will remember my oath of initiation, my oath in the Dalmon Lock, and my oath as a Key Knight, and I will obey them as secret trusts given to me, and if I knowingly or willfully violate any of my several obligations, may I be subjected to all the penalties named. I wish to be and **remain a true** and faithful member of the plateau during life.

All the Knights answer after the C. M.:   He is worthy, let him receive the teachings of the Key.

C. M. to Knights.—Attention, Sir Knights!   Carry swords, form a wall of steel.   (All the Knights, except the C. M. and C. O., are on the lines, and form the wall.)

C. M.—(Resting the point of his sword on the candidate's head.)—By the authority in me vested as Chief of the plateau, I now announce and proclaim that Sir O. W. is now invested with all the rights, privileges and honors that belong to the Uniform Rank of Tabor.   Arise, Sir O. W., and receive the instruction that you need to prepare you for duty.   You are requested to turn and look all around you.   These are your true friends, and form a wall around you as strong as steel; let your friendship be equally as strong.

C. M. to Knights.—Attention, Sir Knights!   Carry swords, present swords, salute, return swords, right-about face, mark time, march to seats.   (The V.-M. leads off in the march, the C. D. M. commands.   They march once entirely around the plateau, and take their seats on the second round.)   The C. M. stands in front of the candidate; the Guards behind the candidate; the C. O. to the right of the C. M., with a large gilded wooden key.

C. M. to Candidate.—Sir Knight of the Uniform Rank, you are now standing in the centre of the plateau of Mount Tabor. This plateau represents the top of the historical Mount Tabor.   About one thousand three hundred years before the coming of the Son of God, the children of Israel were held captives by Jabin, King of Canaan.   For twenty years he oppressed the children of Israel.   Deborah, a prophetess, was Judge of Israel.   She dwelt between Ramah and Bethel, in Mount Ephraim.   The people came to her for judgment. Deborah, being inspired by the Lord God, sent for Barak of Kedesh.   She told him that the Lord God of Israel had chosen him to break the bondage of Israel, and that he must assemble ten thousand men, of the tribes of Naphtali and Zebulon,

on Mount Tabor. Barak knew that it was a gigantic under-
taking to fight Jabin's army of one hundred thousand men
and nine hundred chariots of iron, fully armed and equipped.
This formidable host caused Barak to doubt himself, though
Deborah told him that the Lord God had promised him the
victory. Barak said to Deborah: "If you go with me, I
will go." She said: "I will go with you, but the honor of
the battle shall be given to a woman." The mysterious part
of the scene was the gathering of the ten thousand men on
Mount Tabor. Certain stalwart men of the tribes of Naphtali
and Zebulon were impressed with the idea that they were
wanted on Mount Tabor. These men armed themselves and
silently left their homes, and by different paths made their way
to Mount Tabor. They were surrounded by spies and enemies,
yet they succeeded in their effort to get to Tabor. They were
conducted by the mysterious Key of Universal Power: He
who said, "I open, and no man can shut." When the morning sun come up from the East, the inhabitants of the plains
of Zuanaim saw a sight that filled them with wonder and
amazement. The plateau on Mount Tabor was covered with
armed men, their arms glittering in the sunlight. Tabor the
day before had no living being on its plateau. Where did
this host come from, and how did they pass through our
lines? No one could answer the question. Heber, the
Kenite, one of the descendants of Hobab, went through Kedesh looking for Barak and Deborah; he did not find them.
He concluded that they were with the army on Tabor, and that
the children of Israel were preparing to fight for their liberty.
Jabin's army was encamped on the banks of the river Kishon.
This vast and well-equipped host was commanded by Sisera,
an able general. Heber made haste and ran to the head-
quarters of the Canaanite army, and informed Sisera that
Barak and Deborah had gathered an army on Tabor, and
Israel was preparing for battle. Sisera sent his spies to find
out the strength of the Israelite army. They returned, and

told him that there were about ten thousand. It was a little band compared with the multitude he had under his command. Sisera gave orders for his army to march to Tabor, and to sweep the little band on Tabor out of existence. This mighty host that covered the valleys and plains from Harosheth unto the river Kishon, marched to capture the small company on Tabor. Steadily this large army marched forward until Mount Tabor was encompassed on all sides. Suddenly Barak and his band started on a run down the mount and attacked Sisera's army impetuously. One of the grandest scenes of warfare transpired; the stars of Heaven in their courses, God's artillery of angels fought for Israel that day. Thunder and lightning of Jehovah's wrath was hurled at Sisera's army. The river Kishon overflowed its banks and swept large numbers of the Canaanites into its surging waters. Sisera's army might have conquered Israel, but they could not stand against the Key of God's power. Jabin's host fled, and was pursued by Barak. Sisera was so pressed that he left his chariot, and tried to make his escape on foot. He ran to his friend Heber's tent. He thought to hide there. Jael, the wife of Heber, gave him a drink of milk and hid him under cover with a mantle. He soon fell asleep. The Key moved Jael, and she took a nail and hammer and drove the nail into his temple, which fastened him to the ground. Thus, as Deborah had predicted, the honor was awarded to a woman. When Barak arrived opposite her tent, she called him and showed him the dead general of Jabin's host. Israel celebrated in songs of triumph.

C. M. to Candidate.—Sir Knight, this history that you have just heard, unfolds lessons that we should remember. The first is that the Key of Jehovah's power is universal. He who has the Key to the ineffable name of Elohim is invested with supreme power. Moses received the Key at Sinai, when God appeared to him and said: "I am that I am." Joshua possessed the Key when he commanded the sun and moon to stand still. Elijah held the Key when he caused fire to come from Heaven to kindle the sacrifice. Solomon had the Key when he ascended the throne of Israel. The three Hebrew children were clothed with the Key when they were thrown into the fiery furnace. Daniel carried the Key with him into the lions' den. The prophets and seers held the Key down to Malachi. The sacred Key to the name of God seemed to have been lost when Malachi closed the Book of Prophecies. For nearly four hundred years the world was in moral darkness; there was no direct revelation from God to man. In these dark ages humanity had no guide or light to lead them out of the deep gloom; men felt intuitively that there was a higher power to whom they were accountable. In their earnestness to find and worship this being, they invented all kinds of idol-worship. From time to time eminent men and learned scholars seemed to be inspired to lead mankind out of the gloom, but their philosophic teachings only brought forth a code of morals. They had not the Key of heavenly knowledge. The second part of the mysterious teachings of Tabor is that the higher duties of leading the people to the plains of honor and success are often given to a woman, verifying God's word that she is man's help-mate. In the history of Deborah and Jael this is fully demonstrated. I will now invest you with the Hebrew word, which was used when they lost the Key to the ineffable name of Deity, and the Key of promise that was imparted by the prophet Malachi, that when he came he would make all things new, and the word that closed the old dispensation would open the new dispensation, to continue forever. He who said, "I have the Keys of the Kingdom; I open, and no man can shut."

(The word is given in this form: The C. M. stands by the left side of the candidate, with his right arm across the small of the candidate's back, his hand clasping the right side of the candidate; the candidate's left arm and hand in the same manner across the C. M.'s back. The C. M. and the candidate interlace the fingers of their right and left hand, and hold them up even with their foreheads, in this position the word is given, in a whisper, and the candidate repeats it until he has it.)

The C. M. whispers to candidate.—9–2–5–7–4–5. (The C. M. stands in front of the candidate and gives him the following instruction): The name that you have just received is the Key to Universal Power. It is the sacred Key of Life and Death. The great sign of distress is given by clapping the hands together three distinct times. You are instructed when you hear this sound to find the person who gives it and say: *on the plateau*. If the person answers, *I change not*, it is your duty to defend him if he is in danger, or aid him if he is in want, or advise him if he asks it.

C. M.—THE NEW MYSTERIOUS WORD.—This Key-word was announced at the close of the prophecies, at the beginning of the dark ages. The answer was given nearly four hundred years after the Key-word was proclaimed to the world. It is given in this way: Cross your arms, with the right over the left, and advance and interlace your fingers with my fingers—this forms a double cross. (The hands are opposite the face.) The C. M. whispers 3–8–6–10–1–10–4–6. (The candidate is instructed to answer: The 12–11–6–14.)

C. M.—(Instructing the candidate.)—The crossed arms, with the palm of the hand out, is the calling sign—that will call a Knight of the Uniform Rank to come to you at once. This sign is to be used only when you absolutely need the Knight.

The right hand is the eye in the darkest night. With it the Knights of the Uniform Rank can find a Friend or Brother by day or night. I will now give you a lasting hand of friendship. It is the double bond, that unites the members of the plateau for life. It is the custom when two persons are introduced to shake hands. When you take a hand, clasp it in this manner: with the thumb below the knuckles, and with your left hand clasp the hand of the man that you are shaking. If he is a Knight of the Uniform Rank, he clasps yours in the same manner with his left hand. The first one speaks: Ha, it is you—15–2–6–2–16. The second answers: Yes, of 16–4–14–4–17–5.

C. M. to Candidate.—The Pass-word, which is to be given when you desire to enter an open plateau, is *Calanthe*. This is given to the C. St. In opening a plateau this Pass is given by all who are present. If you should forget it, you will be obliged to retire from the plateau until after it is opened; and then, if a member present can certify that you are a Knight of the Uniform Rank, the Pass will be imparted to you. If there are none present who can certify for you, you must retire from the Mount, unless you can satisfy a committee.

The Test-word is *Dionysius*. This is given only as a part of the opening ceremony.

At whatever place you are, and if you desire to know whether there are any Knights of the Uniform Rank present, you can give this sign: place the thumb and forefinger of the right hand on either side of the nose, between the eyes, and draw them slowly down to the upper lip three times. If any Knights of the Uniform Rank are present, they will answer by drawing the four fingers of the right hand once across the forehead, from left to right.

C. M. to Candidate.—You will please kneel on your right knee. (The C. M. gives four raps, and all stand.)

C. M.—Attention, Sir Knights! Forward march, form on the hollow square, draw swords, present swords. (The C. M. touches the head and each shoulder of the candidate with the point of his sword, and places the point of the sword on the candidate's left side.)

C. M.—I, H. D., by the authority and power as installed Chief of this plateau, do hereby invest Sir O. W. with the full order of Knighthood, with the rank of a Uniform Knight of the plateau. Rise and stand, Sir O. W. (The trumpet sounds, and the Knights clash their swords for about one minute.)

The C. G.'s fasten a sword belt around the new Knight's waist, and put a helmet on his head.

The C. M. puts the hilt of a sword in his right hand and says: With this sword you are to protect and defend a Sir Knight of the Uniform Rank when in danger. You are to draw it in defense of a Sir Knight's wife, widow or children, when they are assailed. With it you are to defend and protect a Daughter of the Tabernacle. You will please salute the plateau and return your sword to the scabbard.

C. M.—Attention, Sir Knights! Carry swords, return swords, to the right-about face, march to seats.

(The new Sir Knight is seated behind the altar. The C. M. takes his seat and requests the C. O. to present the working instruments to the new Knight. The Guards hand the tools to the C. O. and he presents them to the Knight. The C. M. explains them.)

THE EMBLEMATIC KEY.—(This is a large wooden key, gilded.)

C. M.—This is an emblem of the mysterious Key of Universal Power. The name of Him who holds the keys of the kingdom. The keys of life and death. The sacred name of Him who said: "I open, and no man can shut." The key-word that brought salvation and immortality to earth. I admonish you to have faith in His promises, and hope He will open eternal life to you. The key of love will open the door of everlasting bliss, for you to enter.

THE STAR.—(This is a large gilded star with twelve points.)

C. M.—This is an emblem of the Star of Promise. The twelve points represent the perfect number. The morning star rises to usher in the majestic sun which dispels the night's darkness and illuminates the earth with the light of day. It teaches mortals to remember the Star of Bethlehem, which ushered in and proclaimed the birth of Jesus, the illustrious

Light of the World, that spirit of eternal light, and sure guide that conducts His followers through the dark valley and shadows of death to the everlasting light of an immortal life and a starry crown. He said: "I have the Keys of Death."

THE EYE THAT NEVER SLEEPS.—(This is a glass ball, with an eye painted on it.)

C. M.—This is an emblem of the all-prevailing presence of Jehovah. King David said: "Thou art present everywhere." The sleepless eye is the key to the omnipresence of the Great I Am, the Elohim, and of Him who said: "Lo, I am with you, even unto the end." The emblematic eye teaches us to so shape our lives that we may be acceptable to Him from whose perceptive vision the most secret of our heart's thoughts are not hid.

THE EAR.—(This is carved out of wood.)

C. M.—The human ear is an important part of the systematic make-up of mankind. It is the key that opens the door to knowledge and wisdom. The ear receives the instructions which enable mankind, step by step, to ascend to the highest point of art, science, architecture, invention and mechanics. It trains the mind, and enables us to divide the good from the evil. May you receive the good, and banish the evil.

THE CLASPED HANDS.—(The hands are made of wood and gilded.)

C. M.—The clasped hands are emblematic of true friendship—the key that admitted you to this plateau, where the hand of firm friendship clasped yours. The bond that sealed that friendship was woven while you stood in the centre of the solid, compact wall of steel. Every Knight of the Uniform Rank is your friend, and as true as steel. I admonish you to remember the God-man, who is a friend that is closer than a brother.

THE HOLY BIBLE. C. M.—I present you the greatest and grandest of books. It is the inspired word of God, written by God's great and inspired men. It is the mysterious history that holds the key, and opens the door which admits man to enter and read God's will to man. The leaves of this book unfold God's eternal purposes and the future destiny of mankind. I recommend that you carefully read its pages.

THE TWO CUPS.—(These cups are made in the shape seen in the manual.)

C. M.—The key of all wisdom tells of two invisible cups that attend mankind all through his life in this world: The cup of gladness, and the cup of sorrow. These twin cups enter with the birth of man, and are his companions through life.

THE GAVEL OR MALLET. C. M.—This is the emblem of authority, and the proper instrument to be used by the presiding officer. When sounded, it demands attention and silence.

THE THREE EWERS.—(These are made in the form found in the manuel, made of silver, glass or china.)

C. M.—These are used in laying the corner-stone of public buildings—churches, colleges, bridges, libraries, and buildings for public use. They hold the emblems of life: earth, corn and water.

THE BOOK LAWS.—(The constitution and manual.)

C. M.—I present to you the laws and ceremonies that govern our Order. You are requested to read them carefully, that you may be informed of our mode of government.

THE THREE LIGHTS.—(The form of candle-sticks is found in the manual. The colors of the candles are green, white and red.)

C. M.—You see before you the three emblematic lights. Notice that they are burning upon the Temple House. The first is green, and is an emblem of eternal life. The second is white, an emblem of innocence and purity. The third is red, an emblem of blood. The three remind us of the trinity in the Godhead. God, the Father, gave his only begotten son to save the world of mankind. The white represents His purity and innocence. The red represents his shed blood for the redemption of man. He said: "I am the light of the world." He said: "Follow me. I have the keys of death and the grave. They who hear my voice, I will open their graves and bid them rise and inherit eternal life. I have the keys of the kingdom and will open the pearly gates for the faithful to enter into eternal joy. I am He that was dead; behold, I live forevermore." Remember the teachings of the three lights.

C. M.—(Gives four raps, and all stand.)—I now announce that Sir O. W. has been made a member of the plateau and has received full instruction. The C. St. will please enrol his name on the books of plateau No.... (The C. G.'s now conduct him to a seat. C. M. gives one rap, and all are seated.)

CLOSING.

If there is no further business, the C. M. closes the plateau, and he gives two raps, which calls the C. D. M. to stand.

C. M.—Sir C. D. M., the hours grow old, and the time has come to rest from labor. Please notify the C. St. that this plateau will close, and assemble again.................... in the month of...............

C. D. M.—(Delivers the order to the C. St. and returns to his post.)—Sir Chief, the C. St. is on duty, and has received your orders.

C. M.—Thank you. (He gives four raps, and all stand.) Sir Knights, attend, and assist me in giving the signs. (All the signs are given, from the last to the first. In *opening* the plateau all the signs are given, but from first to last.) Sir Knights, attend to the instruction of the Chief Orator.

C. O.—May the blessings of God, the Father; God, the Son; God, the Holy Spirit, be with all true Knights, and all members of the Order of Twelve. May peace and harmony be found in its fullness throughout the length and breadth of our Order, now, henceforth, and forever. Amen! Amen!! Amen!!!

All say: Amen! Amen!! Amen!!!

C. M.—I announce that plateau No.... is closed, to remain so until the..................in month of..................
Sir C. D. M., please give notice to the C. St.

INSTRUCTIONS.

The plateau ought to have one called meeting for drill and practice, at least once a month. The regular meeting is fixed in the by-laws. The C. M. can issue a call at any time. The degrees ought to be given at a called meeting. The regular business at the monthly meetings must be transacted in the Fourth Degree, known as the plateau.

THE BALLOT.

One ballot elects for all the degrees. Those who have received the three degrees, before the Fourth Degree was introduced, are not balloted for again, but are, of course, entitled to the Fourth Degree.

A member is required to have his full dress, sword, baldric, cap, helmet, gauntlet, and brown gloves, within one year after he has received the Fourth Degree. He is required to get these before the expiration of the lawful limit, or stand suspended, until he presents himself in full dress to the plateau in an open meeting. A suspension means a forfeiture of all rights and privileges of the Order of Twelve.

LECTURE IN THE FOURTH DEGREE.

First.—Have you been received on Mount Tabor?

Second.—I am Zebulon, and met Naphtali on the Plateau of Tabor.

First.—How many tribes assembled on Mount Tabor?

Second.—There were but two tribes, under the command of Barak; and Deborah, the prophetess, was our adviser.

First.—How many men were enrolled and prepared for battle?

Second.—There were ten thousand men of Israel, and not a coward among them.

First.—Who was it that betrayed the men of Israel to Jabin's host?

Second.—It was Heber, the Kenite; the husband of Jael, the slayer of Sisera, the General of Jabin's army.

First.—What extraordinary event is recorded in the battle that day between the Cannaanites and Israelites.

Second.—The stars in their courses fought for Israel that day.

First.—What is meant by the stars in their courses?

Second.—It evidently means God's angels. They are often called stars in the Holy Scriptures.

First.—What is the meaning and teaching of the Uniform Rank Degree?

Second.—Its meaning is the highest order of friendship. The ten thousand of the tribes of Naphtali and Zebulon who assembled on Tabor were friends, ready to die for each other.

First.—You have learned well the instruction. Have you the key that admitted you to the plateau?

Second.—I have the first and second. The first is *Calanthe;* the second is *Dionysius.*

First.—You have said well. Can you give me the Key of Life and Death?

Second.—I can, with your assistance.

First.—I will help and assist you. (They meet each other in form and give the ineffable word 9–2–5–7–4–5.)

First.—You have done well. Can you give the mysterious key that binds the old dispensation and the new dispensation together?

Second.—I will try, if you will assist me. (They advance and give the grip. The *Second* gives 3–8–6–10–1–10–4–6. *First* answers 12–11–6–14.)

First.—I am satisfied, but I must test you further. Have you the double token?

Second.—I have, try me. (The double grip of lasting friendship is given. The *Second* gives 15–2–6–2–16. *First* answers 16–4–14–4–17–5.)

First.—You have proved to us that you are a true Knight of the Uniform Rank.

This lecture is brief, made so purposely for the reason that every Knight of the Uniform Rank may commit it to memory. He may be traveling, and may wish to meet in a plateau where he is not acquainted; if he has the lecture perfect, it will enable him to prove his right to visit. The committee will test him by this lecture. The words are figurative. He that is examined must give the plain word.

MISCELLANY.

5—H—9	6—R— 3	14—D —12
4—E—2	4—E— 8	6—R —11
7—V—5	10—I — 6	11—O — 6
5—H—7	1—F—10	12—W—D
2—A—4	10—I — 1	
9—Y—5	6—R—10	
	8—U— 4	
	3—P— 6	

16—K—15	5—H—16
2—A— 2	17—S— 4
6—R— 6	4—E—14
2—A— 2	14—D— 4
15—B—16	4—E—17
	16—K— 5